ISBN-13: 978-1494274450
ISBN-10: 1494274450

Author website: www.loteyrose.com

Going to the Ball

Alice walks toward the two wooden doors at the entrance to the Queen of Heart's ballroom. They are currently closed.

Two guards in powdered wigs holding black polymer spears stand on each side of the door. One of them has a fish-head, the other has a frog-head. Curiously, they're both wearing what look like leather chokers sparkling with red jewels, though it looks unfortunate on the fish guy, since he has no neck to speak of.

Alice is teetering precariously on her high heels as she walks, careful not to trip in the dark. The grinning Cheshire Cat's head is whizzing circles around her, which is making Alice dizzy, and not helping her walking at all.

She shouts, "You're like a gnat! Quit your buzzing. You shall cause me to fall."

His wide grin widens. "My Queen, I daresay your dress is so poofy and wide, it would be impossible for you to fall over, and if you did, it would be like rolling into a fountain of pillows." The black, frilly dress is wider than the kind she usually wears. However, like all her dresses, it has pockets hidden away that are capable of carrying a large number of things—like the Thirteen of Heartless card she carries now. It's a card that can be used to take hearts out or put them in, with the use of a hat. She left her own top hat at her hut, though.

She says, "Are you making fun of me? Are you... taking the *piss?*"

The Cat gasps. "My Queen! You shouldn't talk that way!"

"Why not? My heart is black now. I shall do as I please!" She stops and squinches her eyes at him, staring him down, daring him to contradict her.

He looks down. "Yes, My Queen. I meant no offense. You look quite stunning in that dress."

Alice smiles big. "Well thank you Mr. Cheshire Puss. I'm sure my dress will wow everyone in the Queen's coup d'etat party." A coup d'etat, Alice recently learned, is a French phrase for a violent overthrow of a government by a small group.

Alice nods at the two guards, whom she now stands before and who both seem to be waiting for an appropriate time to break into the conversation.

The Cat's head is hovering in front of the seam of the two doors. He says, "*Afterparty.*"

"Pardon?" says Alice.

"It's technically the coup d'etat *afterparty*. She has *already* overthrown Malice, who is still at large by the way."

Alice rolls her eyes. "I suppose I stand corrected. By the way, you are picking nits, and informing me of things I already know, as if I were some sort of idiot."

"Yes, well you are hardly that. My apologies, My Queen." The Cat bows in that most peculiar way of his, floating in midair and dropping down a few inches while looking down.

The two guards are concentrating on looking off to the sides, minding their own business, but Alice notices them both simultaneously glance at her, then quickly away.

Cor blimey! Minding their own business, my foot! Or even... even...my ass!

In irritation, she huffs, and says to the guards, "Oh, what? What is it, then?"

The guards straighten up to adjust their posture more rigidly. They lower their spears together so that they cross in front of the door.

The Cat swerves out of the way and glides to hover behind Alice like a scaredy cat.

As one, the guards proclaim, "Halt! Who goes there?"

Alice rolls her eyes. "I'm Alice. Everyone knows who I am. The Queen of Hearts invited me here. Here, take a look see."

And she reaches into one of the hidden pockets of her dress. She pulls out her invitation card which is written in red ink upon a heart-shaped card cut from black paper.

The fish guard leans and stares with his fish eyes at it. Alice wonders how he can see properly, since his eyes seem poorly situated on the top of his head and even as he reads, he doesn't quite seem to be looking in the right direction.

Finally the guard gives a fish-grin and says, "Ah, so I see! Begging your pardon for any inconvenience, Queen Alice, for you see, we must take pains to keep out the riffraff."

Alice says, "Oh, I completely understand, for riffraff are humbugs." She gives a royal wave to accentuate her point.

"Yes, quite," the guards both say at the same time.

"We shan't keep you longer," says the froggy one.

"Yes, we welcome you, Queen, and feline guest." That was the fishy one.

They put their arm or fin to the door handle and tug in such a regal fashion, and with such majesty, that Alice almost expects choral majestic sounds of awaaa ah ah, and a brilliant shining light from betwixt the widening entrance, like the shining light of a promenading angel.

The doors creakily open wider—there's no awaaa ah, but at least the light's there, making her squint from the sudden brightness since her eyes were surprised after being in the dark so long. And there is soothing orchestra music for dancing.

The doors are completely open now as Alice gazes at the scene, and the two powder-headed buffoons bow deep and sweep their arms (or fins) in that gesture for Alice to enter, in that way that doormen do.

It is quite awe-inspiring for her, for she had always previously been specifically *un*invited to the Queen of Heart's events.

Not being invited to a party is depressing enough, but to be specifically *un*invited, by being handed an unvitation card that bursts into flames after having read it—well, that was always *particularly* disheartening. *Well, mayhaps I shouldn't use words referring to hearts when thinking to myself, seeing as how mine has recently turned completely black.*

So, it's taking a few moments for Alice's eyes to adjust to the light, but now she gazes—her eyes go wide.

The ball room is a large room filled with various guests and courtiers holding wine and plates of hors d'oeuvres. Their necks all seem to sparkle with some sort of jewelled neck collars. There are pillars here and there, chairs to the left and right sides of the room, there's a table to the right with food and drink. In the back is the dancing area and a winding staircase and to the side of that is the orchestra area. Except now she sees that the orchestra isn't there. That area is empty! And now looking up at the chandeliers, she sees that there are no flames or candles, but there are odd glassy bulbs making light. It's odd, but then, there have been a lot of technological advances in the past few days.

Alice hears herself saying, "Oooh and ahhh," as she gazes.

Next to her, the floating head of the Cheshire Cat states, "My, what a grand party."

Alice says, "Quite," with a nod. Now she begins to compose herself. *Back straight, maintain your royal posture, girl.* She smooths her hands over the top of her dress. *There we go.*

She steps into the ballroom trying to look regal. As she hears the creak of the doors closing behind her, her nostrils fill with the scent of strawberry perfume and chalky wig powder.

It makes her want to sneeze. She suddenly notices someone standing on her right and she jolts from the sudden awareness. She turns her head to see one of the guard cards standing there, with a tiara on his head, holding a black polymer spear. He's one of the diamonds, probably an eight or nine, but she's not interested in summing them, since she is too busy at the moment staring at his tiara.

The card pipes up: "Welcome, Your Majesty, and esteemed kittenous chauffeur."

"Me...ow," says the Cheshire Cate, in a bored, mocking voice.

The card bows deep, and Alice almost raises her hand to hold the card's tiara in place, but it stays quite in place atop his head.

It's a wonder it doesn't fall off.

Alice doesn't know quite how to respond to the card's deep bow. Normally, she might curtsy, but now that she's a queen (technically) such an act might be embarrassing. So, at a loss as to what to do, she falls back on the trustworthy royal wave. She lifts her arm, cocking her elbow at a royally 38 degree angle at the elbow—she holds her hand up, fingers extended, she slowly rotates her wrist, twisting back and forth.

This is mine royal wave, beneath which thou dost withereth, plebians.

The card says, "May you enjoy the afterparty." He bows again and steps aside.

The Ball

I'm so glad to finally be invited to one of these parties. Seems I'm finally part of the in crowd.

Her eyes scan the room. It's such a large room filled with cards and creatures, flamingos and characters. She begins to feel self-conscious about her own naked neck, because all of them seem to be wearing the twinkling collars, all except for the guard cards, who wear tiaras. A few of the attendees she could have sworn she had killed already. For example she sees off in the far end of the room, the Mad Hatter talking to the Queen of Hearts. He's wearing a top hat like usual, though it's obviously different from the one Alice left at her hut.

I wonder if I should kill him again, and maybe this time he'll stay dead, she thinks as she scowls. *But no, perhaps that would cause a scene.* She might have felt fond of him before, perhaps even a little infatuated with him, but that was before her heart turned completely black.

The Queen of Hearts, grinning at the Hatter while he talks, still has her face done up in clown makeup, complete with wild red hair and a ball on her nose—and she too wears a twinkling leather choker.

Alice squints at her because she's far away.

The Queen's face had been transformed by Alice's very own tears a few days ago. *I wonder if anyone has informed her of her facial…situation. Perhaps they are afraid to, lest they be beheaded. Or perhaps she wouldn't even believe them, because when she looked in the mirror before, she hadn't seemed to be aware she looked like a clown.*

The Queen now turns her head to look at Alice. The Queen of Hearts clownishly grins and royal waves at Alice, who royal waves back. Now the Queen begins walking toward Alice, so Alice begins walking too. If they keep walking, they'll meet in the middle of the room. In the middle of the room, there seem to be two people sitting amongst the dancing ballgoers who are blocking her view but Alice sees…

"Cat," Alice says, "is that the Duchess and the Cook?" She points at them. They seem to be sitting on stools across from each other, peering down at a small red table-clothed table in front of them. The Duchess is wearing the striped black and white suit that prisoners wear (and a twinkling collar). She has a black ball chained to her foot, which looks oddly plain in contrast to her dazzling neck adornment. She's never dressed that way before. The Cook looks as he usually does, except with a collar.

The Cat answers, "Yes, My Queen. I do believe it is them. Haven't a clue what they're doing, sitting there whilst everyone dances, though it seems the Duchess would have a hard time dancing with that heavy thing chained to her."

"I quite agree," Alice says with a nod. "Do you think the magistrate finally arrested her?" She chuckles.

"Perhaps so. He always said he would, but had not enough evidence."

The Duchess had always been suspected of child abuse of her were-pig child. Alice had witnessed the abuse first hand. She says, "What do you fathom they're doing? Playing chess?" At this point, the Cook picks something up, shakes his fist and tosses what look to be dice.

"I haven't a clue My Queen. Would you like me to teleport over there to find out?"

"To that, Your Queen says nay. I think it might be bad manners. We shall simply walk."

Alice looks and sees that the Queen of Hearts has stopped to chat with a white flamingo wearing a red hat with a feather in it, with a bandage around his neck in addition to his collar.

It looks a lot like the flamingo Morley, whom she thought Malice had killed. He's looking rather pale, in fact he looks nearly white as opposed to his usual pink hue, but then she expected him to be dead. *Perhaps the paleness comes from having his throat sliced just four days ago. Is his neck wounded? Should he be wearing that collar?*

She shakes her head to clear it.

In any case, the Queen is stopping to schmooze as she makes her way toward me. Ah, I shall have to do the same.

"Cat, with whom shall I schmooze?" She looks about. To her left, with his back against the wall, she sees a giant wingless butterfly who looks a lot like the former-caterpillar-who-smoked-a-hookah, but of course, it can't be him, because he's much too big! Upon closer inspection, he looks odd in another way—he looks one dimensional, like a shadow, except he's in color. Alice keeps looking about.

The Cat begins looking too, saying, "Whom is worthy of talking to, do you think?"

"I don't know." She casts her glance about. In front of her, a little to her right, she sees the Tweedle twins, who recently became melded together to form Siamese twins. "Oops," she mutters, as she quickly looks away to avoid eye contact. She turns to her left. "Let's walk this way, shall we?" Now she sees the knight who likes to invent things, in his black suit of armor with no helmet on—he is talking to a walrus and a man whom she knows to be a carpenter. She is looking at the side of the Knight's body, which is facing toward those he's talking to, and now Alice gazes at the side of his face, which is quite disturbing, since his face is facing the opposite direction from his body and thus facing away from the creature he's talking to. She had been the one who had twisted his head all the way around so that it's now backwards. The lower part of his body is doing fine though, holding a glass of wine and gesturing as he talks to the walrus. The Knight seems to be wearing peculiar glasses with little round pieces of metal held out on the sides. She wonders if his neck is tender from being twisted, for he is wearing a collar too. And come to mention it, so is the Walrus.

"Confound it," Alice mutters.

"What is it?" says the Cat. He turns around and exclaims, "Oh, the Knight! He still doesn't have his head screwed on right!" He chuckles. "I say, what form of spectacles are those?"

"Does no one," says Alice, "in this blasted world, ever *stay* dead? It's a common courtesy to do so."

"Ah, My Queen, I'm guilty as well of not staying dead. Just pray the Knight doesn't ask you to dance. Can you imagine?" He chuckles and Alice giggles.

She says, "I don't imagine you've seen Humpty Dumpty walking about? I wouldn't be surprised. It seems every one else I thought I'd killed is at this party!" She pouts severely.

Alice steals a glance at the Queen of Hearts, who is now once again walking toward the Duchess and the Cook and their game.

"I must admit I'm feeling quite out of place," Alice says to the Cat. "I mean, have you noticed that everyone here except for the cards is wearing a glittering collar?"

As she awaits for a response, she is suddenly startled by an unexpected tapping on her shoulder and gasps as she sees the Tweedle Siamese twins, each with a collar.

The Cat says, "Greetings Tweedles."

"Greetings," says one of the twins, "Ditto," says the other. They turn their attention back to Alice. "Pardon us for frightening you, but would you favor us with a dance?"

Alice stares for a moment at these twins, joined at the chest, with their two heads poking out, two arms at each side. Last she checked, they had a melded arm behind their backs, comprised of two of their arms fused together. In front, they have a leg made of two of their legs combined, so that they seem to be three-legged. And she had been the one who made them that way. She almost laughs at them, but thinks that might be bad manners that would come back to haunt her. Instead she says, "Well I am indeed honoured by your request, but aren't you upset with me, for my role in your... condition?"

"Oh, this?" says one of the twins with a dismissive wave of his hand. "'Tis nothing." "Pish posh," says the other.

"Yes, well of course," the Tweedle continues, "we would love to kill you..." The other twin says, "Agreed." "...but the Queen of Hearts has quite forbid it, so we figure we should at least like to get a dance..." "A shuffling of feet," the other twin says. "...out of it."

One twin says, "So…please?" The other one says, "Yes, what he said." They bow deeply.

Alice thinks they are putting her on the spot and she doesn't appreciate it, but she can't kill them and disrupt the party, but there is no way in the Queen's reign she'll dance with these two buffoons. A sudden bout of wickedness comes over her, so she blurts, "Dance with you?! Well, look at you. They say of bad dancers, 'Oh, they have two left feet.' But do you have two left feet or two *right?* I can't tell?" She raises a brow.

One twin says, "Why you little." He raises a fist. "Stop," says the other, as he grabs the fist, "it's forbidden to harm her."

But now the Cheshire Cat clears his throat in that dramatic manner that one does (despite currently having no neck). "My Queen, the Queen of Hearts beckons."

Alice turns her head to see the Queen of Hearts motioning with her hand, standing behind the Duchess and Cook. At her side is the Mad Hatter and the Knight.

"Ah, my apologies tripodic *gentle*men, but the Queen of Hearts beckons me."

"Cretin," one of the Tweedle twins mutters. "Urchin," mutters the other.

Alice hrmphs and with nose raised in the air begins walking to the Queen. As she does, out in the crowd she thinks she sees the Groundhog talking to a unicorn. The Groundhog looks a bit roughed up with a swollen jaw, and black eye, but he is definitely more alive than she assumed.

"Isn't that the Groundhog?" she says.

"Yes, I do believe it is," the Cat says.

"Pity he's alive."

The Cheshire Cat doesn't say anything.

The last Alice had seen him had been at the entrance to his burrow, where she'd left him for dead.

As they continue walking, the Knight glances at her and hastily departs. Alice now sees that the Duchess and the Cook are seated at some sort of board game—there is a square board with littler squares along the edges. They are keeping their places with little pewter playing pieces that look person-shaped though she is still too far to make everything out.

The Queen watches Alice approach. Next to her stands the Mad Hatter with a scowl on his face. The Queen calls to a guard card who wheels a cart covered with a table cloth atop of which is a large dome cake cover with a mirror surface.

Alice scowls as she reaches the table, remembering all the cruel parties she'd been subjected to before turning 13 a few days ago. "That wouldn't happen to be an unhappy unbirthday cake for me, now would it, for I would find it quite unsettling."

The Queen of Hearts looks aghast. "Oh, my dear uncouth girl, must you be so self-centered? Not everything is about you. Why wouldn't it be *my* cake? I've a cake to be expecting as well, haven't I Tinkerer-poo?"

The eight-year-old girl answers, "That's right Queeny. It's coming later...when I unleash...the festivities."

Alice hadn't seen her before, because she's so short, and had been hidden by the Queen's skirts. The little girl is the Tinkerer, a genius inventor from the outside world who only a few days ago tried to help Malice cross through the Looking Glass into the outside world.

The girl's voice sounded a bit menacing, Alice thinks, but perhaps she's just playing the role of bratty child.

The Queen of Hearts beams at Alice. "Isn't she a marvelous little girl? Why, just in the past few days, she's fixed so many things, invented so many contraptions, even revived a few of the characters you killed." She tsks.

The Mad Hatter nods next to her. "Revived..." he says.

Alice raises a finger, glares at the Hatter, says, "Yes, about that..."

But the Queen doesn't heed the finger, as she continues, "She even invented this game the Duchess and Cook are playing. It's based on our very own Wonderland. She's always working on something."

Now the Duchess says, "Yes, and you're interrupting. I happen to be winning. Shhh..."

The Queen of Heart's eyes go wide. "Shhh?! Tinkerer, hit that mute button of yours."

The Tinkerer is holding a rectangular device. "Indubitably," she says, pressing a button on it.

The orchestra music suddenly shuts off, making it seem eerily quiet in the aftermath. The crowd of dancing ballgoers groans disappointedly. That device must be one of her many inventions. A few days ago she had used the March Hare's watch to speed up the "place time" of Wonderland, causing technology to advance at an astounding rate.

The Queen glares at the Duchess. "I've made it quieter so you can hear me loud and clear. I've no intention of *shhh*ing. You are just a Duchess—you don't shush me. You're lucky I didn't have you beheaded rather than merely shackled, jail bird."

The Duchess gulps and nods, looking meek.

The Queen says, "Now resume your game, whilst We chat with Alice here."

So the Duchess picks up the dice and rolls them with her hands shaking, and moves the little pewter piece that looks like her, complete with ball and chain.

Alice is peering at the board. "What is this game called? Why, looky, Hatter!" She points. "There is a square labeled "Grimm Game!" What happens when you land on it?"

The Hatter rolls his eyes, says, "Yes, I am quite capable of reading. As to what happens, ask the Tinkerer."

The Tinkerer says, "The game is something I created in order to meet my goal. I call it The Hunting of the Snark."

At the mention of the word, the Mad Hatter straightens up and looks about with mad eyes. "Snark?" He hisses through clenched teeth. "Where?!"

"Do you see it?" the Queen teases with a little laugh. "I know you keep looking."

The Hatter looks about for a few more seconds, even doing a little twirl, before giving up. "Yes, ever since I was resurrected I've been determined to find the Snark myself. I've studied up on it, trying to get inside its head, you see. Maybe a little too much, as some of the snarkiness seems to have rubbed off on me."

Alice intends to get to the bottom of how the Hatter was resurrected and *what* exactly a snark is and *what* is "snarkiness", but she only manages to utter, "How—" before the Tinkerer cuts her off, impatient at having the attention drawn from her.

She says, "Yes, the Hatter inspired me in the fashioning of my brilliant and endlessly entertaining game. It should become a household staple."

Alice leans over and peers down at the board with her fingertip pressed to her lips to be respectful to the Tinkerer. "What use is a household staple if there is only one? You could only staple one thing and then the game, as it were, would be over?" She reads some of the squares— Humpty, Tweedles, Tea Party, Troll's Riddle, Knight, Duchess & Cook. *Duchess and Cook?!*

"Yes," says the Tinkerer, "I construe the meaning of your joke. It's a pun, isn't it?" Her voice sounds as if she had just rolled her eyes prior to her utterance.

"Looky," Alice says while pointing. "Wait, joke what joke?"

The Tinkerer sighs. "Perhaps I give you too much credit. But I must be more forgiving if I am to think of you as a sister, as I might."

"Hmmm?" Alice says while still pointing, "Why, Hatter, that square has Tea Party on it. That's what you're known for. Pray tell, what happens when you land on it, do you know?"

The Hatter shrugs. "Perhaps I finally end the game by finding the Snark? I've been looking for it." Now he too peers down at the board. "Is there a square marked Snark?"

The Tinkerer says, "The nature of each square is top secret, known only to me. When one lands on the square, or any square, one will be given the directions and abide to the challenge of the square."

Alice, sounding puzzled says, "But once anyone lands on a square, the secret will be known. How can it be a staple in every household once all the secrets are known?"

The Queen of Hearts now says, sounding miffed, "Yes, and more importantly, why is there no square marked Queen of Hearts? Perhaps I should demand a square?"

The Tinkerer says, "Do not doubt me, for I am the Tinkerer. I anticipate all. I *control* all. Why, look at all the people at this ball wearing my cat collars, all the cards wearing my tiaras. I'm what is called a person of influence." She leans toward the Queen of Hearts and stage whispers, "And perhaps it's best you shan't go wanting for a square. Might be more trouble than it's worth, if you know what I mean."

"Very well," the Queen says, in an almost meek way.

Almost meek! What strange power does this Tinkerer have? I am awed and a bit afraid myself!

The Tinkerer says, "In the short time I've been here, my accomplishments have been great, my resurrections numerous, my influence unprecedented. Why, it was because of *my* fashion sense that everyone in the court now requires one of my glittering cat collars to be *in* fashion." She nudges her head at the Queen and Hatter. "Lest, one should come to be *out* of fashion." And here, she nudges her head at Alice, now the Cheshire Cat. "I mean, ewww. How could you even *wear* one of my cat collars, despite being a cat, since obviously you refuse to don a neck? I mean, what is that? How rude!"

The Cat says, "You'll forgive me I hope, for lately whenever I attach my body, it ends up being forcibly removed. And am I rude? I've looked over your board game, and I see no square marked Cheshire Cat. Why is that?"

The Tinkerer waves her hand dismissively. "Oh you shall find out soon enough. But first, I need to fill you in on my numerous accomplishments and inventions, so that you all may be suitably impressed. There are so many, I don't know where to begin." To Alice, she says, "Have you any ideas?"

"Yes," says Alice. "Did you revive the Hatter? This is the second time I've thought him dead when he wasn't." She pouts.

The Hatter crosses his arms and hrrmphs. With nose raised in air he says, "You might want to worry more about reviving your hair. It wants a cutting and conditioning."

The Queen of Hearts chuckles. "Good one."

The Tinkerer and Alice both roll their eyes at the same time.

The Tinkerer says, "Yes, after you paralyzed him from the neck down, I was able to figure a way to get him up and moving about, though the solution was less than ideal. However, it was less of a challenge than the Knight. Why, you snapped his neck as well, correct?"

"Yes," Alice says, "but he was asking for it. I saw him earlier, wearing some contraption on his head."

"Yes, he's out there somewhere. Well, after you turned his head completely around, I gave him a set of glasses with mirrors on the side so that he can see behind him, you see. It's just a temporary solution. Speaking of mirrors, I've invented a special coating that makes one-way mirrors, as well. That's what the cake dome is covered with."

Alice says, "It just looks like a regular cake cover."

"With a mirror surface…" says the Tinkerer.

"Yes…" Alice says, her brow crinkling. "And?"

"And with a one-way mirror, someone on one side can see through it as if it's glass, while someone on the other side only sees a mirrored surface."

"Oh! Is there someone tiny inside there, watching us, then? The Butterfly perhaps."

"No, silly, the Butterfly is over there." She points. "Surely, you can see him, as large as he is." The group turns to look at the large wingless butterfly against the far end of the room. Many of them gasp, Alice included, as the insect suddenly swells to twice its size!

The Tinkerer giggles. "Sorry, couldn't resist. I pressed the magnify button on my invention I call a remote control." She's holding up the rectangular box with all the buttons.

"How did you make him grow like that?" Alice asks.

"Yes, how?" says the Cat.

The Tinkerer says, "My dear, it is merely a visual trick. I developed a camera for the Caterpillar that magnifies his image and projects it against the wall there, so that he could participate in the ball, kind of, without feeling so tiny. Not the best solution, but it'll have to do. After all, I'm more interested in fixing his wingless problem."

Angrily, Alice says, "You'll give him wings?! But I cut his off!"

"Well, I will soon equip him with the ability to fly better than he would have with wings, but giving him a wing transplant is a possibility . Hmmm…" Her eyes roll up to the top of her head for several long seconds.

They watch her expectantly. The moment goes a little longer than comfortable.

The Tinkerer says, "Oh, I was thinking of the Knight and his neck, wondering if I could give him a neck transplant. No, I do much prefer my original regimen for his neck problem."

"Yes, well you never said what that was," Alice says.

"Oh? Didn't I? Well tomorrow he shall start his treatment. I've developed braces for his neck!"

"Like ones for teeth?" Alice says.

"Yes, quite like that actually. The brace will be connected to his neck, and slowly it will be turned a little bit, so that eventually, his head will be turned all the way back around again! Isn't it brilliant? And speaking of the devil, there he is. Hey Knighty poo!"

About twenty feet away, the Knight turns and looks afraid as his eyes rest upon Alice. He shakes his head.

The Tinkerer says to Alice, "Why don't you wave at him and see what happens."

Alice snarls. "I wouldn't like him to be around me again. I'm likely to snap his neck again for good measure."

"Oh, he won't come. He's quite terrified of you. Come on, wave. It might be funny…"

So Alice raises her arm up in the air and at the Knight, royal waves, which is a way of waving she has in which she holds her open hand pointing up while slowly rotating it back and forth.

The Knight shrieks and covers his eyes. His body, which is facing the other way, runs awkwardly away, to disappear amongst the crowd. Here and there his presence is made known by the jostled shoulders of those he's run into and the clanking of his armor.

"You see," says the Tinkerer, "ever since you snapped his neck, the poor chap has developed parthenophobia."

"Which is?"

"A paralyzing fear of little girls!" She raises her hands to cover her mouth as she unleashes a giggle explosion (figuratively).

Alice smirks and laughs, as do a few of the others.

The Hatter says, "And to think, some people are afraid of snakes. Bloke doesn't have his head screwed on right."

Alice says, "He right well should be afraid of me. And to think, he thought his piddly 'inventions' were better than yours!"

"Hardly," the Tinkerer says, with no doubt whatsoever. "I can do anything ten times better than him. I always succeed and never fail!" Her face screws up in utter little-girl determination.

"Well," mutters the Queen of Hearts, "there is the matter of…"

"Of what?" the Tinkerer says, barely managing to control her rage.

"Of Malice. You said you would bring her to me."

"Yes, well, I shall of course, I just haven't gotten around to it. I think you should increase your gratefulness and decrease your impatience. I mean, look at all I did for your rinky-dinky ballroom. I wired it so it could use electricity, thanks to the Red Queen," she gestures upward at the odd chandeliers without candles, "invented the light bulb and put them up there, hooked up the sound system to play phonograph records of music." She presses one of the buttons on her remote control. The sound of the orchestra blares for a few seconds before she mutes it again. "And *this* is how you thank me?!" Her face is turning red.

The Queen of Hearts looks thoroughly rebuked, hanging her clown face in shame. "My apologies, Your Royal Inventor, it's just that I so wish to behead Malice, because she coup d'etated me."

Malice, who is Alice's heartless twin/reflection and nemesis, had taken charge of Wonderland for a while, before the Queen of Hearts regained her throne. Alice isn't sure who of the two is worse.

The Tinkerer waves her hands. "Yes, yes, I know, I will get to it. I've had so many things to do, but I'll get to it."

The Queen of Hearts merely keeps her mouth shut and does the whirly hand motion with a bow that means *Please, by all means, commence with what you were saying.*

The Tinkerer commences, "Yes, where was I? So, I invented so many things. Fixed so many of the characters—the Knight, Flamingo, former-Caterpillar, Hatter of course, am I forgetting anyone?"

"Humpty Dumpty," Alice offers.

The Tinkerer's mouth turns down slightly in a smidgeon of a frown. "Oh, yes, him. Well, I've been working on a solution to that puzzle. An algorithm. But that shall wait till later. Anyone else?"

The Cat says, "The Jabberwock."

"Ah!" The Tinkerer squeals and claps in delight. "His fate shall remain a surprise to be revealed later! Speaking of surprises, I think it's time to reveal what is beneath this cover!"

The Queen now squeals. "My cake!"

With a grin, the Tinkerer says, "Mayhaps, mayhaps." She presses her palm to the handle of the cover. "Come, gather around, so that we shall all see." And with a dramatic lift she reveals what's beneath the cover.

What's Beneath the Platter?

Underneath, is the severed head of a Jabberwock with blue and red wires sticking out of it here and there and leading through holes down into the lower part of the cart. He's wearing a leather headband adorned with sparkling red jewels. The decapitated head bulges its eyes, opens its mouth, and proclaims, "Ta da! I'm baaaack."

Alice lets loose a little eek of surprise. "He's alive! But I thought I killed him!"

"You did," says the Jabberwock. He wriggles his muzzle as if he wants to nod, but since he has no neck to nod with, he has to be content with just the muzzle wriggling.

"You did," the Tinkerer says, "but it turns out Jabberwock heads are remarkably resistant, and they take a long time to rot too. So since the Jabberwock's head was still fresh, I was delighted by the results of some experiments I tried. I was testing theories I had read about electro-stimulation. I hooked some wires into some key areas of his brain and zapped them using electricity I had stored in a battery, thanks to the Red Queen, and voila! He started blinking and talking, just as if he had never died in the first place. Unfortunately, his body didn't respond to the electro-stimulation. Well, it flopped around a bit like a headless chicken, but was really quite useless. But it doesn't matter, as I've been working on a replacement body for him."

Alice says, "But you fixed the Hatter when he was paralyzed. Could you not use the same method with perhaps a bit more stitching?"

"Oh, pish posh. What do you know? *I'm* a genius and *you* are not. Keep that in mind. So, in any case, now you see the usefulness of the one-way mirror coating I invented. Was it a good view, Jabberhead?"

He says, rolling his eyes toward her at the edge because he can't move his head, (no neck)—"Oh yes, quite. Like looking through clear glass, it was."

"Excellent. Good to know my test case was successful. But let us move on to the next festivities. I have a hard time sticking to one thing, in case you haven't noticed. We shall soon let *her* eat cake," with a side nudge of her head at the Queen of Hearts. "Are there any other of my amazing inventions and revivals I have left out?" She ponders a few moments.

Helpfully, Alice offers, "Humpty Dumpty. He even has his own square in your board game, I see. But I haven't seen him out and about around here. Surely you haven't put him together again…*have* you?" Both of her eyebrows she feels rising dramatically.

"Oh, no, he's still all broken up, the poor little guy. But it's on my to do list. I've been perfecting the algorithm."

Alice's face scrunches up in annoyed puzzlement. "Although…rhythm?"

"No no, algorithm. But let's save that for later. It's one of the many surprises I have planned, and segue!… speaking of surprises, the Queen of Hearts shall soon have her unbirthday cake, but first, pardon me for… elongating the suspense…"

Alice mutters to herself during the pause, "You use such big words for such a little girl."

The Tinkerer sniffs. "Well, yes, I'm *only* a genius. But you are the beautiful Queen Alice. I look up to you. You should not go bare necked during the rest of this ball so…" she tries to snap but fails. "Sorry, I need to practice my snapping." She claps. "Chop chop. Guard cards."

"Yes," the Queen of Hearts shouts. "Off with their heads!" She looks around, looking a bit dazed.

"Oh, no no, Queen. I was merely trying to get the cards to present her with—oh never mind…" She presses a button on her remote control. She says,

"Guards, bring forth two cat collars of marvelousness."
A guard card comes forth presenting sparkling collars.

The Tinkerer takes a collar in her hand and says, "These collars are so fashionable it hurts." She smirks, which Alice finds odd. "I present it to you Alice, so that you may not stand out from the crowd."

Alice squeals and claps in a blur, so excited to be a part of the cool crowd. She lifts the collar up, turns, and lets the guard card lock the clasp.

Everyone else in the little group who have hands clap as Alice preens.

"And now," says the Tinkerer, "I'm going to ask, though I can already predict the answer. Mr. Cheshire Cat, will you materialize your body so you may have a neck on which to don a cat collar?"

He says, "My apologies, little one, but bad things happen when I have a body. I respectfully decline."

The Tinkerer says, "Isn't it ironic that you're the only cat, and yet the only one not wearing a cat collar or head band?"

"I suppose it's ironic, yes."

"Never mind. As I said, I anticipated your response, and so I have prepared another honour for you. Guard card!" She snaps—this time she actually succeeds in snapping her fingers, though it *could* be louder. She looks pleased with herself for snapping.

A guard card rolls forth a trolley with a plate of shredded plant material on it.

The Cheshire Cat sniffs the air and proclaims, "Catnip!"

"That's right," says the Tinkerer, "Yes, please, help yourself! Partake in its exquisiteness!"

The Cheshire Cat merely says, "Yes," then the floating cat head seems to lunge at the plate, his tongue happily lapping at the curious confection known as catnip.

The Tinkerer says, "So now that you all have been sorted, let's commence with the rest shall we?"

Alice watches the Tinkerer press two buttons on her remote control.

Alice looks at her and is instantly wracked with searing pain through her whole body—the pain is most intense in the area around the collar. She screams, but that only makes the pain worse and within seconds, she realizes that any movements she makes will bring more pain, and so she does her best to remain perfectly still.

Alice hears and watches as all the others in the room shriek and seem to reach the same conclusion, including the Hatter, including the Queen of Hearts. The exceptions are the guard cards, who simply watch it all happen.

It's like a game of freeze tag, if freeze tag was enforced by a pain collar!

Out of the corner of her eye she is aware of the Cheshire Cat who now seems surrounded by a semi-transparent green dome of light. He is butting his head against it quite perturbedly, proclaiming, "I say, what is the meaning of this! It's witchcraft!"

The Tinkerer says, "No, Mr. Puss Puss, it's merely a little something I developed called a containment field. If my calculations were correct, you shall find yourself unable to pop in and out of places in that annoying manner you have."

The Cat smirks. "We'll see about that." But he doesn't disappear. Now he's scrunching his face up and grunting with effort. Still doesn't disappear.

The Tinkerer giggles. "See?"

"You little brat! Let me go this instant!"

"Oh, no no, you don't get to order me around. I need you contained in the field—it is a most astounding creation of mine, it keeps you from bending space in that manner you do. I figured out how you do it, and utilizing energy particles that spin in the opposite direction, I was able—"

The Queen of Hearts shouts, "Nerd! Shut up! You can't coup d'etat me!"

"Au contraire. You see, I just did."

The Queen of Heart's face screws up in rage. "Guard cards, seize her! Off with her head!" Her arm moves a little, but that causes her to scream in pain. She is panting, making sure to stay still.

The Tinkerer makes a condescending pout at the Queen of Hearts, now says, "They will no longer follow your orders. You see this button here?" She holds the remote control out. "When I press it, it activates the control tiaras."

"The tiaras control them?" the Queen says.

"Not exactly. See the guard cards have very simple brains. I was able to invent a device that controls the loyalty center of their brains. I disguised it in the tiaras. When I press this button, they all will follow my orders, and *only* mine."

There are gasps and muttering.

The Queen of Hearts says, "So you're taking over, is that it?"

"Well, I needed you all controlled, for the sake of the game."

"What game?" shouts Alice.

The Tinkerer glances at her. "Why, The Hunting of the Snark. Everything depends on what happens during it. But you shall see soon enough. But now it's time for a treat. I do believe I promised the Queen of Hearts cake?"

The Queen's eyes widen, her mouth twists. "I don't think I want my cake. Haven't had supper yet. Wouldn't be proper."

Again with the condescending pout. "But I promised. I feel I've promised you so many things that I haven't delivered. For example, I promised to bring you Malice and so I shall." She attempts to snap, but fails this time. A mild look of annoyance, then she says, "Bring on the cake!"

The tablecloth flutters and a lanky, thin girl rises up from under the table, and shouts, "Smushy in your face!" as the child, who looks exactly how Alice would look in a cat suit and mask, pushes a piece of chocolate cake into the shocked Queen of Heart's clown face. The girl smears it all about the white clown queen's face as she has to stand there and just take it.

Despite the seriousness of the situation, Alice can't help but giggle a little.

The girl says, "Surprise! Unhappy unbirthday! The Tinkerer snuck me in under the table just for this moment. And now, with *her* help, I, Malice, shall be the new ruler of Wonderland! Ah, it's good to be Queen."

Alice watches as the Tinkerer pulls a tube from her dress pocket, presses it to her mouth and blows a dart into Malice's bottom.

"Eeek!" Malice shouts as she swats the dart away. She turns to look at the Tinkerer, glares, then her eyes roll upward, her head tilts backward and she collapses unconscious to the ground.

"Ha!" shouts the Queen of Hearts. "She gets what she deserves."

The Mad Hatter sniffs. "She had a short reign."

Alice sighs. "So why'd you go and do that, then?"

"Well, I needed her subdued for the sake of the game, which will commence shortly. You and Malice are to be opponents."

"Why? It's just a game, right?"

"Oh, no, Alice. It is everything. But you need only wait and you will see, but as of right now you can't. See, that is." She snaps, and grins proudly. "Now that was a proper snap! Guard cards! Blindfold Alice."

And one of the guard cards covers her eyes from behind, while a cloth slips over her mouth and she smells the all-too-familiar scent of formaldehyde.

START

Alice stretches and yawns. It is just another day—she must prepare herself for the long hours of being humiliated and hurt by the citizens of Wonderland. But wait, didn't I kill them all, or was that all a dream?

Blearily she opens her eyes.

Hey, this isn't my bed.

Now she remembers the Queen of Heart's ball. *Or was that a dream too? Probably not, since I'm wearing my poofy black dress and high heels.* She checks her neck—no collar there.

In a daze, she gazes around. She is lying on the hard ground—beneath her is a floor made of what looks to be pure blackness. Malice is lying a short distance away in her cat suit, either dead or asleep. She doesn't have a collar on either.

A pair of oversized dice lies in front of Alice. Beyond that she sees a perfectly straight line of glowing green in the floor, and beyond that, she sees the Tinkerer standing, watching her. On one side of her is the Cheshire Cat's head, floating unhappily in the floating semitransparent green sphere of the containment field. On the Tinkerer's other side is the Red Queen. (Who, by the way is *not* the Queen of Hearts and they would each be offended to ever be considered to be the other.) The Red Queen is doing her usual routine of constantly running in place, except there is now something different beneath her feet. It is some sort of contraption—it is as if the ground beneath her is moving, allowing her to stay in place—and the contraption has steel bars rising up to provide handlebars for the Red Queen to hold onto as she runs. A red beam of light shoots out from the bottom of the contraption into a clear crystal block on the ground.

And the Tinkerer and Cat and Red Queen are all standing (or running) on a floor of utter blackety black, that stretches forever. The surroundings are all black except…she looks around, except the glowing green lines that form a perfect square of about 15 feet by 15 feet around her. Alice notices there is a word on the ground in red lettering, but she can't read it from here.

The Tinkerer's voice booms, louder than Alice would have thought possible, as if her voice is amplified somehow, saying, "Do rouse Malice, won't you dear? You've been knocked out for a few hours from your perspective, but I've been using the March Hare's watch and it's literally been days and days for me. Of course,

I've been inventing lots of things, but now, I've waited long enough."

"Why should I rouse her?" says Alice defiantly.

"Well, because let's get on with it, that's why. You know the containment field I used on your cat? Well, the green lines of the square you're in operate on a similar principle. The green lines mark the boundary for you. They mark where the force field is. It may look clear, but it is like clear glass, only much much more powerful, so you cannot cross the green lines. And Malice will either wake now or later. Let's not make this more difficult than it needs to be…"

Although there's a chance the Tinkerer is lying, Alice very much doubts it—the Tinkerer has created so many astounding inventions that she seems now quite in control of things.

I suppose I'll rouse Malice, because at least misery loves company, aye?

She crawls over and prods Malice with her fingertip. Now she notices the letters on the ground next to Malice spell, "tart".

Poke me again, and I'll snap your neck, Malice thinks. She hears Alice's voice saying, "Wake up, Malice, we've a predicament on our hands," and so Malice opens her eyes. She sees the black square with green edges, sees the dice, and the Tinkerer and Cat and running Red Queen outside the square.

Wobbily she stands and stretches and yawns. "Well, this is different."

Alice now sees the word on ground is actually "Start".

The voice of the Tinkerer booms, seeming to come from every direction at once. "So good of you to join us, Malice. Oops, let me adjust the volume. Okay, Malice, you'll be groggy for a while from the knockout juice, but that shall soon wear off. Another one of my inventions I created in my spare time. Now the blowgun on the other hand, wasn't my invention. I got the idea from adventure periodicals. It's rather simple for my tastes. But it's effective."

Malice shouts, "You knocked me out with a blowgun?"

The Tinkerer rolls her eyes. "You're sharp. About as sharp as a butterknife."

Malice makes a fist. "You know what else is sharp? My razorblade." She feels along the outside of her thigh.

The Tinkerer says, "It's not there. All your weapons have been taken away. I did let Alice keep the Thirteen of Heartless card, though. It may come in handy later."

Malice scowls. "How about I come over there and punch you in the face, you little squirt! Come on Alice, we can take turns punching her." She cracks her knuckles and begins walking toward the Tinkerer.

Behind her, Alice says, "Sounds like a jolly good show!" She too cracks her knuckles and follows behind.

But as Malice tries to step over the green line, she grunts as she slams into something solid, her masked face smushes against it as if it is glass and with a staticy sound a wall of green, semi-transparent energy flashes. It disappears as instantly as it appeared when Malice steps back. "Ah!" She rubs her nose. "What was that?"

The Tinkerer begins giggling. "Why it's like you just walked into a glass door! Ha! But, unluckily for you, you wouldn't be able to break through. It's a force field, similar to the one around the Cat—it's to keep you in your squares as you play the game."

"What game?" Alice shouts.

The Tinkerer seems preoccupied by something. "Hmm? Oh, The Hunting of the Snark, of course. You're on the start square. I say, that knuckle cracking noise you two made. Does it hurt?"

"Sometimes." Malice and Alice both say at the same time. They look at each other and scowl at each other.

While staring each other down.

Malice says out the side of her mouth while still staring at Alice, "But it never really hurts that much."

"Yes," Alice says, glaring deep into Malice's eyes, "the pain's over quick. Like a snapping of a neck." She narrows her eyes at Malice. "You probably wouldn't feel it at all."

"Now now," says the Tinkerer, "no killing your opponent. You'd forfeit the game. You wouldn't want that. Trust me." Her eyes roll up and her face scrunches up a bit as she seems to think. "You know, I think I shall try."

"Try what?" Malice says with a snarl.

The Tinkerer doesn't reply. Gingerly, she presses her fist into her other hand and tentatively presses.

LOTUS ROSE

Alice rolls her eyes. "You've got to do it quite harder than that."

Malice says, "Yes, much harder."

The Tinkerer presses her fist harder, but there is no sound. She tries her other fist. Still no sound. Her hands drop to her side and she frowns a little and looks at them with big sad eyes.

Malice suggests, "Perhaps if you punched yourself in the face, your knuckles might crack, then."

The Tinkerer lifts her hand and snaps her fingers. She beams proudly. "Can you do it?"

"What?" Malice says. "Punch you in the face?"

"No, snap your fingers."

Malice says, "Yes, but I would very much prefer to punch you repeatedly in the face, until you're bloody."

Alice adds, "And I would like to make a game of it and see if I could break every single bone in your face."

The Cheshire Cat joins in. "And I would like to chop off your head and stick it in this containment field."

The Tinkerer huffs and turns her head to the Red Queen. "How about you, Queen?"

"Don't interrupt me! Can't you see I'm running?!"

Malice says, "Can we just get on with this, then?"

Alice says, "Quite right. Tell us about this game of yours."

The Tinkerer's face screws up and she folds her arms. "Fine then. But you needn't be rude to the gamemaster, which is what I am. After all, I designed this whole game just for you two. You could at least be grateful."

Malice folds her arms in a mocking mimick. "Well, what, pray tell is the prize in this wonderful game of yours?"

Self-consciously, the Tinkerer lowers her arms. "That's a surprise. But it's a well and proper prize indeed. Would you like me to explain the game to you?"

Malice says, "Okay, but first might you explain why the Red Queen is running and the Cat is contained beside you?"

The Tinkerer giggles. "The Red Queen is running and running and staying in the same place. I designed a treadmill for her."

Malice scrunches her nose. "Treadmill?"

"It's a machine for exercising," the Tinkerer explains.

"And she must exercise here, pray tell why?"

Alice chimes in, "And where exactly *are* we anyway? Is this still Wonderland?"

The Tinkerer answers, "I need her here, because it's her running that makes all of *this* possible."

"How?" Alice asks.

"I've devised a means of transferring her kinetic energy into electric energy. I originally stored the electricity in batteries, but now I found out I can do much more. Now I convert her energy into a laser beam, which is a concentrated beam of light, and shoot it into the special prism. The light that comes out, I then reflect into the Looking Glass."

She points to the bottom front of the treadmill, where a red beam of light is shooting out into a small clear object about five feet away. The Looking Glass is nowhere to be seen.

She continues, "In other words, her running keeps all the lights on. Of course, I must be careful with the laser and make sure not to walk through it, or let your shadows fall upon it. Since you're Alice and Malice, your shadow is special and would disrupt the laser. Oh, why am I even bringing this up? Your shadow left you, anyway. So, you asked where we are. We are in Wonderland, yes, but we might as well be in an entirely different world of dreams, where reality can be shaped by the will of a creator, me. Watch." She presses a button and suddenly the black of the square transforms into an oversized replica of the Start square of the board game that the Duchess and Cook were playing in the middle of the ballroom. The floor is even now made of cardboard.

Malice and Alice gasp and look around, struck speechless. The green lines are still there on the edge and the area outside them is still pitch black.

The Tinkerer explains, "The square around you is like a square on the board game. Using a system that combines electricity and technology with the dream-energy of hosts, and the special reflection characteristics of the Looking Glass, I have been able to create what I like to call 'virtual reality'—it is an illusion really, but unlike an illusion, you can feel, hold, even smell the objects inside the square. The process taps into the same method the Cat uses of warping space using the form of physics peculiar to Wonderland. I like to call it nonsense energy. The Cheshire Cat didn't realize that's what he was doing. He merely wished to teleport himself, and poof!—he did. Of course, I couldn't have him popping in and out everywhere as he pleases. That would quite ruin the game don't you think? So I had to contain him." She tilts her head toward him.

The Cheshire Cat head looks woeful as he says, "I am imprisoned, having been charged of no crime."

The Tinkerer tsks. "He's quite a charming kitty. I thought I would borrow him for a while, as my little pet. It's too bad I can't pet him or anything, and he's a bit odd, because he refuses to show his body, but at least he can't scratch me. And he is absolutely, most definitely *required* to stay by my side."

He mutters, "Young miss, if it meant I could scratch your eyes out, I would gladly reveal my paws."

The Tinkerer shrugs in delight. "See? Isn't he most clever? Won't you purr for me, my kitty kitty?"

The Cat snarls. "Go to hell, brat."

"Now now, my pet. Sticks and stones…"

"You're just lucky I'm in this containment field."

The Tinkerer rolls her eyes. "Anyway, let me explain the game to you…"

Malice clasps her hands together in mock delight. "Oh, *shall* you?"

Alice laughs derisively in support, but her attention is taken away as she ponders the Red Queen, who continues to run and run atop her treadmill, *whatever that is. Does she never grow tired? And why does she always insist on running? Some sort of compulsion perhaps? Or is it anorexia? A need to be skinny?*

The Tinkerer says, "So the game is called, The Hunting of the Snark. The goal is to find the Snark, but I can't tell you how to do so. The board which are on is comprised of squares. You will roll the dice to decide which square you land upon. Each square presents its own challenge, created by me. It shall be a marvelous contest, don't you agree, pitting one blackhearted girl against her heartless mirror reflection and seeing who is best suited and adaptable? There are prizes on the squares or you may also be rewarded with a certain amount of points—let's call them 'quids' for the sake of understanding, because you may have the opportunity to buy things with your points. I have personally designed each square and challenge. Using the virtual reality, all the settings and objects will be indistinguishable from reality. However, I can only use the virtual reality to create inanimate objects. So let me assure you, that everyone you meet shall be quite real. I have used various methods to persuade them to… participate. And that is all the instruction I shall provide. And I shall entertain no further questions."

Malice raises a finger and says, "I've a question…"

"Okay, fine. But this best be the last."

"Fine back at you. I can't help but wondering, seeing as how I'm about to become a playing piece in a board game…what, pray tell, exactly is the point of this?"

The Tinkerer answers, "It will all become clear in the end." She claps. "Now let the game commence! You shall each pick up a die and roll it, to see who goes first."

Malice and Alice both realize they have little choice, and they both realize the folly of attacking each other, but Malice the Heartless and Alice the Blackhearted can't resist taking verbal jabs at each other as they each pick up an oversized six-sided die.

"You," says Malice as she shakes the die, "are going to lose, and lose horribly."

Alice says, "I don't think so, cat girl."

"Nice outfit," Malice says sarcastically. "It would make a good funeral gown."

The Cat shouts, "Catfight!"

Alice rolls her eyes. "Whatever, heartless hussy."

"Blackhearted harlot."

"At least I *have* a heart."

Malice pouts a little. "You're not so great, you think you're so great."

The Tinkerer says, "Okay. Roll the dice already! And make sure it's a proper roll or I shall disqualify it. I'm the referee, savvy?"

Malice and Alice shoot hate-filled glares at each other, before Malice lifts the die above her head and with a shout hurls it with all her might towards the Tinkerer's head.

With a soft thud, the die hits the force field which flickers green with a staticy sound before going invisible again. The die bounces off and rolls along the ground.

The Tinkerer grins. They all peer at the die to see that it has landed on 4.

The Tinkerer says, "I like your enthusiasm. Okay, your turn Alice."

Alice sighs. "Come on, six!" She launches the die into the air by pushing it away from her chest. It hits the force field, rolls, lands on 5. She gnaws her lip. "So I shall go first. I don't know whether that's good or bad. How does this work? I see no other squares."

The Tinkerer, with a smile intones, "It works like this." She presses a button and Malice and the start square disappear.

Now Alice is standing on a small black square, outlined in green. A bunch of plain black squares lie ahead of her. They all have plain words on them—they are laid out in a big square like the board game. The Tinkerer and Cat and running queen are still there a short distance away.

"Roll the dice if you please," the Tinkerer says. The dice have shrunk to regular size.

Alice picks them up and rolls a 2, a snake eyes. That's usually bad luck.

The Tinkerer says, "Now simply hop forward two times. You see that square marked Troll's Riddle?"

"Like hopscotch?"

"Quite. When you land on the square you'll be able to see the virtual reality inside of it."

Alice prepares to ask where Malice is, but as she gestures with her arms, her hand hits a force field at the edge of the small square.

The Tinkerer explains, "I shrunk the square so you can hop. It's open on the front so that you can hop to the next square."

"Ah, I see. But where is Malice?"

"She's still here, but you just can't see her. And she can't see you. Neither of you will know what the other is up to unless you land on the same square. Now, won't you take your turn?"

"I doubt I have much choice." She mumbles, "But first," she removes her heels, puts them in her dress pocket. "I shall go barefoot. Well, here goes," and she hops forward past the square marked Humpty, onto the one marked Troll's Riddle. Ahead is a square marked Tea Party.

When she lands on the square marked Troll's Riddle it grows to a size of about 20 feet by 20 feet.

The virtual reality begins to kick in, sprouting and growing.

The Troll's Riddle

The scene begins to fill in, inside the 20 foot by 20 foot square. First the outlines of objects appear, followed by the colors being filled in, as if this *virtual proclivity, or whatever it's called,* is one big colouring book.

So now she is standing on a square that shows a portion of grass-covered ground—of course it is just a small portion that fits in the square, outside of which the Tinkerer, Red Queen and Cheshire Cat are watching.

She sees the outline of a large man standing on her right. Next to its feet is a freshly dug grave with a wooden cross sticking out. She can't tell whose grave it is, though, since so many had recently died.

Why, he must be 20 feet tall. She takes a closer look as the details begin to fill in.

Why that looks like the combat mech I was in a few days ago!

Indeed it does—it's like a giant suit of armor made of metal and material called plastic. It holds a large pistol in one hand and a flamethrower in the other. But it has a deformed head, different than how she remembered.

Just a few days ago, Alice had been inside one that had looked just like this one from the neck down. She had stood inside the cockpit, which was in the stomach area of the combat mech. She'd worn a helmet that let her see from the combat mech's eyes, and she'd been connected by wires and sensors, so that each movement she made was copied by the machine. She'd used its flamethrower to tend a garden.

I wonder if this is the same one, and if someone's inside, she thinks as she glances at the stomach area, but the cockpit is closed and she can't see inside.

The combat mech isn't moving, and perhaps it would be best if it didn't.

The Tinkerer says, "It's your combat mech!" Once again her voice sounds amplified.

Alice keeps her eyes on the looming machine, wary for any signs of movement. Now that all the details have filled in, she can see that the head of the machine is in the form of an ugly troll's head—a metal one. She finds herself crouching down, despite herself. "Pray tell, what is the meaning?"

"I have designed each square to pose a challenge. And getting past the combat mech is your challenge. You must pass the test to get your prize." She points, and Alice now sees that behind the combat mech, resting on the ground in the grass, there is a treasure chest, just like the kind that gets sunken in pirate ships.

How silly!

Alice says, "What's in that, then?"

"Catnip!" the Cat shouts.

The Tinkerer says, "It's a secret my dear. First you have to pass the challenge."

Alice makes a show of looking dramatically about. "I say, is all of this real? Or is it the illusion…or… virtuousity?"

"Virtual reality," the Tinkerer corrects.

"Is the grave real? And whose is it?"

"It's a copy of the actual grave with the body of someone who I shan't reveal right now."

"Yes, or is it the…that…is the suit real?"

"You are not actually at the actual location. That is not *actually* the grave or the *actual* combat mech. They're both a fact simile."

"Fact simile?"

"Fat smilie!" the Cat shouts. The Tinkerer glowers at him and he cringes.

The Tinkerer says, "No, no. A *facsimile*. It's a copy. Like I said, all the inanimate objects inside the squares are illusions, with a few exceptions. But all the *living* beings are real. But I tried to make my facsimiles as close to real as possible, to limit confusion, and keep things fair. Well, sometimes I may have embellished things a little." She points at the troll head.

Alice is feeling quite annoyed by the Tinkerer, but she realizes she has little control of the situation. "I see," she says. "So let's not draw this out any longer. You say the inanimate objects are 'facsimiles', and all the living beings are real. But I see no living beings, but I can't see inside the cockpit of the combat mechy. So who's in there, and what's the challenge?" She puts her fist on her hip.

The Tinkerer shuts both eyes while grinning at Alice for several seconds. "There is someone inside the suit, who is a part of the challenge that you must overcome."

Alice, truly puzzled, cocks her head to the side. "What was that?"

"What was what?"

Alice says, "You closed your eyes for several seconds before speaking. Surely, you're too young to have a stroke…"

The Tinkerer's face scrunches up in a comically exaggerated manner. "I didn't blink. I *winked*—that's when you close *one* eye while keeping the other open, moron."

Alice laughs. "Yes, while I concur on your definition of a wink, that is most decidedly *not* what happened. You most assuredly did *not* wink. You blinked. And I do not bear false witness."

The Tinkerer says, "Shut your face!"

"I concur," says the Cat. "You did most definitely *blink.*"

The Tinkerer scowls at him. "I thought I told you to limit your utterances." She presses a button.

The Cheshire Cat yelps in pain as a staticy sound and flash issues from his containment field. He mutters, "Still a blink…"

The Tinkerer harumphs and stamps her foot. "Still," she says, "winking is not so easy as some might imagine. I can hardly be faulted for failing in the endeavor, as young as I am." She turns to the Red Queen, who is still running. "I implore of you, can *you* wink? It's not so easy after all, what with your running at the same time…"

The Red Queen, who is still running, huffs, but makes the effort to wink and does so easily, followed by making a tchh sound click with her tongue.

"Oh, fiddle sticks," the Tinkerer mutters.

The Red Queen says, "There, I did it, now will you leave me alone? I'm running here! I'm trying to get somewhere!"

The Tinkerer makes a dramatic show of cupping her hands in front of her mouth to form a hand-megaphone. "You're going nowhere! Nowhere in a hurry!"

The Red Queen crosses her arms as she runs, an impressive feat. "Well, imagine if I *didn't* run. I imagine I'd end up going backward."

The Tinkerer stares at her, dumbfounded. "I say, you're quite unpleasant. You're only useful for your electricity. I'm done talking to you."

"The feeling's mutual, and you know, I *would* leave but your containment field is keeping me stuck on the treadmill."

"Yes, well, suck it up, and keep moving forward!"

The Red Queen hrmphs.

The Tinkerer smooths her dress and rocks back and forth upon the balls of her feet. "Ladies and gentlecat, the suit's function is to guard the treasure chest. It is armed with numerous deadly weapons. The suit has an occupant...whom you must defeat to get to the treasure chest. If you are killed—"

Alice gasps. "Killed?!"

"Yes, if you are killed or can't get past the guard within the seven minute time limit, you will fail the challenge, and you won't get the prize. And your turn will be over."

"Can a facsimile kill me?"

"Oh, yes. It can do a proper job of it too. I hope it doesn't happen though, because the game has barely begun. So, would you like to know who's inside, then?"

Alice mumbles, "It hardly seems fair. They've got a combat mech and I'm just a little girl."

"Behold! Inside the suit is..." She presses a button. The panel covering the stomach area of the suit slides up. "...the Jabberwock!"

Alice now sees the Jabberwock's head inside the open cockpit. The head is wearing goggles and is suspended by wires connected to various points of his scalp.

Alice says, "Well that's rather garish."

The Tinkerer says, "I think you mean ingenious. Come, I shall unfreeze him now." With a push of one of her buttons, the suit begins to move, slightly, looking about.

With dread, Alice waits for him to shoot or pummel her. But he doesn't even seem to notice her.

"He can't see you yet," the Tinkerer explains. "In the virtual reality, I control all that he sees, all that he hears, even what he smells." She beams. "Marvel at him. Isn't it amazing what I've done! I told you I would give him a body and I have. And now he can move around and shoot things."

"Yeah, but it's only a facsimile."

At this point the Cat chooses to interject, "He didn't invent bodylessness, you know."

The Tinkerer, ignoring him, says, "It may be a facsimile, but it's a replica of the actual suit in the nonvirtual reality, except for the head part. It works outside the virtual reality too, trust me. I've done my best to recreate everything in Wonderland in my game, with a few exceptions of course."

"So that's really the Jabberwock in there?" Alice says.

"Yes, yes, and as far as he's concerned he's back at his usual spot, guarding the chest, like I told him to, as payment for his new body."

"What of his old body?"

"That old thing? It's obsolete. It's buried—see the grave? Now, before I start the challenge and the countdown, I do have a clue for you."

"Of course you do."

"Er yes, and your clue is…

"To get past the floating jabberhead,
And win the chest that with prize is filled,
You must make him to the world be dead,
In a way in which he is not killed."

Alice says, "My, what a curious rhyme. How can he be made dead if he shan't be killed? Suicide perhaps. Hari kari again?"

The Tinkerer shrugs while smiling. "Oh, this shall be fun!" She presses a button and points at the air. Alice sees green numbers appear in the air that say 7:00, now 6:59…It's a countdown of the time she has, she realizes.

The troll head of the combat mech turns to look at Alice, and, inside the cockpit, the Jabberwock's mouth opens wide in joyous surprise. "Mother?" The amplified voice booms from speakers located in the suit's mouth.

Alice looks behind her, now points at herself questioningly.

"Yes, you. What are you doing here, Mum?"

Alice looks to the Tinkerer. "What's he talking about?"

The combat suit follows her gaze.

The Tinkerer answers, "I've modified the virtual reality to make you appear just like his mother in his eyes."

Alice smirks. "And now you've let him know. Does that forfeit this square?"

"Who are you talking to, Mummy?" the Jabberwock says.

"Silly little mama," the Tinkerer says, "he can't hear me or see me. He can hear you, though. But your voice is her voice, as far as he can tell."

"Mum?" the Jabberwock in a combat suit says.

Alice wonders why the Jabberwock doesn't notice she's smaller than his mother would be, but she realizes his sense of proportion might be off since he has a new, larger body.

Alice turns to look at him. She doesn't know whether to look at the Jabberwock head in the cockpit or the machine's head. She chooses the machine head. "Yes, dear?" She smiles.

"What are you doing here? You came to visit me, right? Because I hope you didn't come to get the treasure. I'm guarding it."

I have to play it careful here. "Well, what if I did come here for the treasure?"

"Well then, I'd have to kill you if you tried to get it, even though you're my mother. I promised to guard the treasure for the Tinkerer, because I owe her for giving me a new body."

Maybe it's not worth risking my life to get the prize. "What is the treasure anyway?"

The mech suit shrugs. "I don't know. I just have to guard it. I've been guarding it and guarding it without sleeping. I'm so tired." At the mention of his tiredness his eyelids droop sleepily. "Oh, how I've missed you. Don't let me fall asleep, okay?"

I wish you would fall asleep, that way I could get past you to the treasure.

Alice glances at the suit's weapons. She has no idea how she'll be able to defeat the Jabberwock without any weapons of her own. "Why don't you just go to sleep, then I'll keep watch. I'll wake you up in a few minutes okay?"

"Uh, sorry Mummy, the Tinkerer specifically told me I can't sleep. I can't stop guarding the treasure until I am relieved of duty, not even for you, Mum."

Alice rubs her chin and tries to think it through. *This square is a puzzle to be worked through. Perhaps the Jabberwock himself has given me a clue. The Tinkerer made me appear like the Jabberwock's mother. But why? Maybe the Jabberwock is bluffing and wouldn't harm or stop his mother from simply running and grabbing the treasure. But no, that hardly seems a satisfying solution of the clever sorts of puzzles the Tinkerer is fond of.* She watches as the Jabberwock head yawns. The suit's metallic troll head mimics him but the suit doesn't really have a mouth, though.

"Cover your mouth," Alice scolds.

"Sorry Mummy." And the mech suit covers the mouth it doesn't really have.

Alice taps her chin with her index finger. *And what of the clue—I must make him dead to the world, but not killed.* She watches the Jabberwock yawn again, this time his suit covers his mouth. He says, "Mum?"

That's it! If he falls asleep, he'll be dead to the world, but he won't be killed!

Alice says, "Would it really be so terrible for you to sleep a little while? I'll guard the treasure for you."

"Yes, it would be terrible. Whenever I sleep, my suit shuts off, so I don't go destroying things in my sleep. Even the automatic weaponry shuts off."

"Automatic weaponry?"

"Yes, think of it as like a reflex. If you were to suddenly run toward the treasure for instance, my gun would automatically lock onto you and fire, or say, if you tried to hop into the cockpit and kill me, the combat mech might punch you or maybe even self destruct."

"Self destruct?"

"Yes, an explosion of the suit's nuclear generator that would kill us both. Any act of aggression might set it off. So watch yourself. I should have warned you earlier. Be gentle." He chuckles. The suit holds its arm over its belly while Jabberhead and Trollhead laugh. "Sorry, I'm a bit loopy from the lack of sleep."

Alice snaps her fingers. *I've figured out why the Tinkerer made me look like his mother!* Mustering up a stern voice, which for some reason she thinks must be made low, she says in the deepest low voice she can muster, "Jabberwock, my son, I *order* you to go to sleep this instant. For I am your mother, you see."

The Jabberwock chuckles. "Oh, Mummy, you know that never worked. That's why you always did the other things…"

"What other things?"

"Oh, come now, don't tease. You know, the kiss and the song, the bedtime stories about eating people."

"Oh, yes, that's right." Anxiously she looks at the countdown numbers. 4:11.

Alice thinks now of her own mother, of being tucked in, kissed goodnight—and how that would put her to sleep. *Perhaps that's it! If I am gentle, the suit's automatic systems won't be activated. Giving him a slap or strangle might bring an explosion. Running for the treasure could fill me with bullets.*

But a good night kiss?

It would hardly be a kiss of death, though it just might well make him dead to the world.

She doesn't have much time. "Lower your suit thingy. I want to get a closer look at you."

"Why?"

For a moment, Alice is at a loss for words, but now, she recalls her own mother's behavior, and shouts, "Because I said so, Jabberwock!"

He hesitates, as if he's a child deciding whether to defy his mother. "Very well," he says.

The mech suit kneels, its knees churning into the grass.

I must sooth him to sleep. Take advantage of a child's obedience to his mother, a child who is afraid to disobey.

She peers. "My, what a lovely cockpit."

"Yes, it provides me control of my new, superior mechanical body."

"Yes, so you have a new toy, is that it? But what of your dear old Mum, who raised you, who spent 26 hours in labor."

"26? I thought it was 12."

"Silence!"

"Sorry."

"Have you no respect? I suppose you don't care about me anymore. I, um, changed your diapers, right?"

"Yeah."

"I tucked you in at night?"

"Yeah."

"Yeah? Yeah?! I don't think you even remember. Tell me, um, what did I do, at night, you know, after tucking you in, to make you go to sleep? I bet you don't even remember!"

The Jabberwock head pouts—she can't see if the the machine troll head tries to mimick him. "Of course I remember!"

"So tell me, then. I want to hear it from your lips." She puts on a stern face.

The Jabberwock's face looks meek. He doesn't draw his head back as he seems to want to, though. "Don't you remember? I would always have trouble going to sleep, and you would warn me that if I didn't, then you wouldn't give me how-to-kill-little-girl lessons the next day. But if I did go to sleep, then in the morning we could have little girl barbecue ribs for break-her-ribs-fast. But if I still couldn't go to sleep, you would do it, remember?"

Alice tries to play along and sound convincing. "Of course I remember, the thing that would make you fall asleep in…"—she looks up to see 3:03—"three minutes? What did we use to call it?"

He pouts. "The little-girl's-goodbyes. Don't you remember? They would put me to sleep every time!"

Alice chuckles. "Oh, yeah, that's right." While this whole time she has no idea what he's talking about. *Little-girl's-goodbyes?*

"Yes, I loved your songs so much, Mummy. I'd ask you to sing one right now, but I'd probably go to sleep!"

Alice gasps, because it suddenly clicks in her mind. *Little-girl's-goodbyes sounds like lullabies! His mum would sing to him about that?* Her stomach lurches a little. She tries to keep smiling, but she feels it's a bit plastered on her face. She suddenly wonders what she looks like through the Jabberwock's eyes.

The Jabberwock continues, "Speaking of little girls, I was recently decapitated by the little girl Alice. Oh, I would very much like to hear a song about *her* dismemberment and killing, that's for sure. But no, I'm on duty. Promise you'll do it when I'm not on duty, Mum? For old time's sake."

Alice groans inwardly. *He deserves to have his head cut from those wires for how he just talked about me. But…no, I must try to pass this challenge! That's the more important matter.*

She looks at the clock. Two minutes left!

Her eyes ping from side to side. "How about a lullaby about killing evil doers or nobility. Or the Queen of Hearts even! Would you like that?"

His face screws up. "No, I wouldn't. Did you not hear me?! I was quite recently decapitated by Alice. *Decapitated!* If there is any time more fitting for a little-girl's-goodbye, I don't know when it is, but wait, what am I talking about? I'm on duty!"

As Alice glances again at the glowing numbers, she is aware that her time is limited, but still she lashes out for alternatives.

She says, "I find this machine fascinating. Why, if someone were to try to kill you or poke out your eyes?"

"The automatic defense system of the machine would make swift work of them, and if I were killed, the suit is set to auto destruct with an explosion."

Alice imagines grabbing the Jabberwock head and running off, carrying it like in a game of rugby. "What if someone grabbed your head and tore it from those wires and ran off?"

"It would be interpreted as death. Big explosion."

Alice sighs. "What if you went to sleep?"

"When *I* sleep, the machine sleeps, unfortunately. That's why I have to stay awake."

Alice scowls and glares at the Tinkerer. *You set this up!* Alice knows the Tinkerer probably can't read her mind, but nonetheless, the Tinkerer winks back.

She sees she has one and a half minutes left! She has no time to play around anymore if she wants to win the prize, whatever it is.

The Jabberwock's eyes have taken on a faraway dreamy expression. "Remember how you would do it? You'd tuck me in and sing the little-girl's-goodbyes and then kiss my forehead and boop! I'd fall right to sleep. You, remember, huh? Do ya?" His eyes droop a little. "Oh, I wish—but no, must stay awake."

The clock is literally ticking, and Alice is frantically searching her mind for any lullabies about killing little girls—the closest she can come is, "Rock-a-bye Baby", about babies dropping from trees. *Hmmm. There's "Ring Around the Rosie", but that's not a lullaby is it?*

Outside the square, the Tinkerer taps an imaginary wristwatch. Alice's black black heart is pounding hard in her chest. "Quick, what are the lyrics of your favorite little-girl's-goodbye?"

He grins and winks. "Come on, don't tease me. You've teased me enough already. Okay, I get it, I haven't visited you in so long you've forgotten everything, yeah yeah I get it."

Alice groans. *I don't have time for this.* She hops and scrambles into the cockpit. She begins cooing while smiling soothingly. She moves closer to the Jabberwock head, which says, "What are you doing, Mummy?"

"I'm gonna sing you a new song. About killing Alice. Would you like that?"

"Oh, yes, yes." He doesn't nod, because he can't. "I mean, no, Mummy! I can't fall asleep." He doesn't shake his head.

"Young Jabberwock! You shall do as I say, because I am your mother! Now I shall sing you a new song and you will listen, and not interrupt."

He cringes. "Yes, Mum, but I won't go to sleep. I'm sorry, I just can't. I promised."

Alice softly caresses the Jabberwock's cheek with the back of her hand, while trying to think up some lyrics. His cheek feels very smooth and cold. "There, there, shhh… Errr…" She awkwardly tries to sit him in her lap by getting beneath him and raising one leg and manages that for a few seconds before going into a crouch. She pretends to tuck him in.

And now she starts to sing while gazing deep into his eyes.

And now she sings.

Rock-a-bye Alice, swinging from a noose.
When the wind blows, the knot will come loose.
When the knot slips, her body will fall,
And down will come Alice, black heart and all.

The Jabberwock sighs with a goofy grin—his eyelids droop. Alice kisses the cold flesh of his forehead. His eyes close completely, as Alice's heart shudders and twitches in protest of the kiss.

Alice doesn't waste time. She hops from the cockpit onto the ground and runs to the treasure chest. She tries to fling open the lid, but it's locked.

The Tinkerer shouts, "Congratulations! You passed the challenge!"

Alice looks up to see that the clock has stopped at 16 seconds.

The green grass beneath her feet promptly disappears, and is replaced by pure black. All that's left in the square is the treasure chest and the word Troll's Riddle on the ground.

Alice puts her hand on her hip. "Hey, how do I unlock this thing?" she says, as she notices a strange warm twitching sensation in her chest she had been too excited to notice before.

The Tinkerer says, "Bear with me, I am inspired. Listen now, to the chronicle of your adventure—my poem I call,

~*Jabberwonky*~

'Twas realish and the virty tech,
Did shimmering, appear,
All trolly was the techy mech,
With tummy-head, so queer.

Beware the Jabberhead, my girl!
The guns that shoot, the flames that flare.
Beware lest 'lectric jolts unfurl,
And launch you through the air!

Beware the booby traps attached,
If you touch him the wrong way,
For more deadly than a bandersnatch,
Are nukes that blast and flay.

She took the Jabberhead in lap,
Not ready yet, to die.
And caused the head to take a nap,
With tuck and lullaby.

And so beauty put the beast to bed,
And thus did pass the test,
The sleeping head, to the world is dead,
The prize waits in the chest.

Alice bows. "Well, thank you for that. I feel quite epic! Might I open the treasure chest now?"

"You're welcome, and certainly." She presses a button.

Alice opens the chest and peers at a metallic object on the bottom—it's a metal heart shaped like a cartoon heart with a knob on the side for winding it, like on a watch.

Alice notices that her *own* heart is racing and feels odd —quivery—she feels a little dizzy. She presses her hand to her chest to feel her heart twitching and spasming, *but at least it's still beating*. Her chest feels warm to the touch, which is odd, but she puts it out of her mind. *It must be all the excitement.*

Alice looks to the Tinkerer, says, "What is it?"

"It's one of my inventions. I call it the Ticktock Heart. Speaking of hearts, how's yours feeling?"

She says, "It's feeling a bit odd, actually. Did you do this?"

The Tinkerer lifts her hand to her chin and rubs it, mutters under her breath, "Curious." But since her voice is amplified, it is loud and clear.

Now Alice's face scrunches up. "*You* did this!"

"Hmm?" She glances up from the ground. "Oh, yes, quite so. I know that your heart had gone completely black and you would have loved nothing more than to kill the Jabberwock all over again…"

"Yes, but your silly game prevented it."

"Yes. I arranged the game to make you do something against your blackhearted nature. You had to be warm and soothing to win. I like how you cooed."

Alice's scowl deepens.

The Tinkerer says, "So what you're feeling must be your heart's reaction."

Alice crosses her arms. "It's like I'm allergic to kindness!"

The Tinkerer chuckles. "I wonder if it's fatal?"

"If I could get to you right now, it'd be fatal…for you."

"Yes well, too bad I control the game, isn't it?"

Alice's heart has gone back to normal. "Well, my heart feels okay now, no thanks to you."

"Yes well, now you have won the Ticktock Heart. I assure you, it's not one of the illusions. It's the real thing. Would you like to exchange it with your organic heart?"

"Could I do that?"

"Well, yes, I believe so—we are in Wonderland after all, but you'd have to use that card of yours, but you need someone else to play the card game with or you can't make it work, right?"

Alice nods. "That's right. And I'd also need a hat."

In mock pity, the Tinkerer says, "Oh, too bad."

"And I think I couldn't be bothered to wind it."

"Oh, you need only wind it in the beginning. After that, it winds itself, using the movements of your body, you see. Self-winding gears—one of my inventions."

"But why would I want a ticktock heart anyway? What would it do for me?"

She rubs her chin. "I haven't tested it yet, but I designed it to not only be a heart, but to provide enhanced computational capacity to the brain."

"Huh?"

"It would make you more intelligent, like having an extra brain. I theorize it would make someone less emotional and more analytical and precise, like a machine."

Alice puts her fist on her side. "Well, why the heavens would I want that?"

She shrugs. "Well, maybe the heart you have now is faulty. You said so yourself."

"But at least I'm not a nerd like you. Do *you* have a ticktock heart?"

"I don't believe so, but as I've never seen it, it's theoretically possible. Perhaps if I used the x-ray monocle…" She's muttering to herself.

"What monocle?"

She looks up from the ground. "What? Oh. Never mind. Enough of this. Your turn is over. Time for me to attend to Malice."

And pressing her remote control, she disappears, leaving Alice alone in the plain black square labeled "Troll's Riddle".

A Grimm Game

"Whoo!" says the Tinkerer as she and Red Queen and Cat suddenly appear outside the Start square. "Wasn't that last square exciting! It would make a right and proper chapter of a book, it would!"

Malice rolls her eyes. "Well you better be quicker next time—I shan't be kept waiting."

The Tinkerer snarls. "You are in no position to make demands. However, you may roll the dice, if you please."

Malice crosses her arms. "Hrrrmph. And what if I *don't* please."

"Well, then you shall forfeit your turn. Eventually you would likely lose. Come now, don't be defiant. Just roll the dice, love?"

"Bah, don't call me love. I hate that word."

"Interesting."

"What was that?"

"Nothing. Go on then." She waggles her hand at the dice.

Malice gives forth a dramatic sigh before bending to pick up the dice and tossing them forward.

She rolls a 3 and a 4 for a total of 7. The square she's standing on goes completely black with a glowing green edge, now it shrinks to the size of a hopscotch square, and squares appear in front of her, all with labels. She hops forward 7 times—past Humpty, past Troll's Riddle, Tea Party, takes a right turn, goes past Groundhog, Shadow, and Butterfly then takes a right turn onto the square marked, "Grimm Game". As she lands, the square expands again to a square about fifteen feet on each side. Colours and shapes begin to fill in. She sees three humanoid creatures sitting on what look to be stools in front of her. The Tinkerer and companions are on her right.

She can't tell who the three guys are, because the details aren't filled in, but as the seconds pass, the details become clearer.

She is inside a pub. Well, partially—the inside of the room, with its tables and bar—table, extends only to the edge of the square.

Sitting on the three bar stools in front of the bar are three cute teenage boys—they all look between 17 to 19 years old. They seem not to notice her—are looking right through her.

Malice says, "This is a most curious pub."

"Why do you say that?" the Tinkerer asks.

She sweeps her hands about. "It hasn't any walls."

"Yes, well it's a virtual pub."

"And," Malice adds, "it hasn't many customers. No surprise, considering its lack of walls." She points at the three guys. They have similar features. *Perhaps they are brothers,* she thinks. Again, they don't seem to notice her—they look bored, even.

And Malice knows it's impolite to point, but she's trying to get *some* sort of rise out of them, so she waggles her finger and says, "Nuh uh uh," as if chastising them. Still no response.

The Tinkerer explains, "They can't hear. I control all that they see and hear within the virtual reality, so I've decided to make them not see or hear us for the moment, so that we may speak freely before the challenge of the square." She giggles. "Think of it as if they are in a sound proof booth before the commencement of a television dating game."

Malice places her hand on her hip. "Isn't that anachronistic?"

"Not at all, love. Place-time has jumped forward in Wonderland."

"I *told* you I don't like that word."

"I know. I did it on purpose, because it is what this square concerns itself with." She sticks her tongue out at Malice.

"Love?! Phooey! And *why* may I ask, did you virtually realitize me in a bar? You know, me mum would never allow it."

"I know, and that's exactly a good reason to do it! Don't worry, I'll keep your secret from her." She winks.

Malice screams in exasperation while lifting crinkly claw hands up. "Argh! I cannot stand!... You!"

"I know."

"I wish I could wring your little neck." She makes a pantomime of choking a neck.

"I should like to see it," the Cat adds.

The Tinkerer says, "Yes, well, that's not gonna happen, so let's focus back on the game."

Malice tries the silent treatment, crosses her arms and looks away.

The Tinkerer says, "Those three boys are the Brothers Grimm..."

Malice can't help but raise her eyebrow and peek at them for a few seconds, but quickly goes back to ignoring—with her nose raised in the air.

The Tinkerer says, "I know what you're thinking. Yes, they are the very same brothers behind the fairy tales. And yes, they are much younger than you'd expect them to be. Well, it's complicated, but they managed to open up a portal and ended up in Wonderland, where they ended up falling in love with a girl very much like you."

Malice decides to give up the ignoring routine, but keeps her arms folded as she looks at the Tinkerer. "*Must* you keep mentioning the word?"

"What, 'love'?" Her eyes crinkle as she smirks.

Malice unfolds her arms. "That's the one."

"Well, yes, I must, if I am to present your challenge."

"Which is?"

"All in time. First, I'd like to present the prize. And I assure you, it's the real thing, not a facsimile..." She presses a button on the remote, and a circle opens in the floor in front of Malice. A pedestal slides up with a metal object on top of it.

Looking down at it, Malice sees that it is a black metal gauntlet like from a suit of armor, adorned with glittering red heart-shaped rubies and inscribed with ornamental engravings and an odd, repeating symbol. It is smaller than for a full grown man—it might fit a child. It actually looks as if made for a girl, but what girl would be allowed to own and wear such a thing? It wouldn't be proper.

"Behold!" the Tinkerer proclaims. "The Vorpal Fist!"

"Vorpal? Like the Jabberwock's sword?"

"Quite."

"What is that symbol?" she asks as she leans in for a closer look. The symbol, repeated numerous times on the fist, looks like a broken heart inside a circle with horns on top.

"It is a corruptagram, which symbolizes a girl's wicked heart, which is appropriate, for it was a girl who donned it long ago."

"A girl?"

"Yes, a girl they came to call, 'the girl who will tear your heart out and show it to you before you die'!"

"Ewww! And second, that's a rather long name. Did she have one shorter?"

"Yes, but I'll leave that out."

"Why?"

"It would complicate things. Now, as to the Vorpal Fist—"

"Where's the rest of it?"

"What do you mean?"

"There's no suit of armor? That's what I thought when I first saw it."

In a chiding tone, the Tinkerer says, "Noooo…there's no suit. It's not meant to be armor. It's meant to be a weapon."

"Oooh. A weapon." Malice nods and her eyes go wide with wonder.

The Tinkerer nods back. "Yes, it was forged in ancient times by no one knows who. Soooo… anywhoo… it is a powerful weapon with a special power. Some say that it was forged with metal mixed with the crushed hearts and tears of the heartbroken, and when it is donned…"

"Yes?" Malice realizes that she is standing on her tippy-toes, and goes flat-footed.

"Like the girl in the past, when you put it on, it seeks out the hearts of others, tears it from their chests and kills them."

Malice gasps. "That's so amazing."

"Yes, it is a nearly irresistible weapon, but…"

"But what?"

"But it can only seek out and tear out the hearts of those who still hold love in their heart for the person wearing it."

"Oh, wow. How cruel." A wicked grin creeps up Malice's face.

"Yes, it is indeed, and that girl I spoke of, she used this weapon on the three brothers and upon many others, which is how she came to be called…"

They both take a deep breath, now they speak together the name in reverential recital:

Quoth the Tinkerer:

"The Girl Who Will Tear Your Heart Out And Show it To You Before You Die!"

Quoth Malice:

"The Girl Who Will Rip Your Heart Out and Shake It at You Before Smushing in Your Face. Then You Die!"

The Tinkerer arches a brow. "You were a bit off, but it was your first time."

Malice shrugs. "I took poetic license. Wonderland is *supposed* to be poetic right? So how do I win this woesome weapon?!"

"It's simple. You must figure out which of the three Brothers Grimm still loves you and use the Vorpal Fist to tear out his heart."

Malice murmurs, "And smush it in their face like cake before they die. Wait, what do you mean," she makes air quotes with her fingers, "*still* loves me?"

The Tinkerer nods. "That's right. One of them still possesses a heart filled with love for you."

"But I've never met them before."

The Cat adds, "And plus, you're too young for boys."

The Tinkerer ignores him. "Yes, you think you've never met before, but in a way, you have, because I can control the virtual reality."

"So, what, you wiped out my memory of meeting them?"

"No, no, you haven't met them yet. But, no, what I mean, is that I control their perceptions, and when I turn on their vision and hearing of you, you will look and sound exactly like that girl they remember from the past—the girl that all three brothers fell in love with and fought over. But only one of them still truly loves her, because only one still has a heart. The other two are heartless."

"Curious. Tell me, who exactly *are* these three brothers anyway? I thought there were only *two* Brothers Grimm."

"Only two *famous* ones."

"Well, regardless, I've never heard of them being in Wonderland..."

"That's because they've been locked away in the Queen of Heart's dungeons for unleashing troublesome fairy tale characters. They are actually very powerful and important blokes, tied into the fairy tale magic of old. But none of that pertains to the challenge of the square right now. The important part is this: when the Queen of Hearts was coup d'etated, I went through her things, such as her collection of hearts, and her dungeon of prisoners. That's where I found the Red Queen."

The Tinkerer points at the running Queen before continuing, "I also found the three Grimm brothers in the dungeon, still alive, but all three were heartless—that girl that they all loved had torn *all* their hearts out. And they died for it, but were revived. But let's keep the story simple. Amongst the Queen's collection of hearts, I found two hearts of interest. One heart was Humpty's and there was another one that was clearly labeled. It was one of the brother's hearts, that had been ripped from his chest by the girl and her Vorpal Fist. The heart was still red. How it came to be in the Queen of Heart's collection, I am not privy to know, but I do know that I was delighted at the puzzle it presented to me. As you may well know, I have a long standing interest in medical procedures."

Malice nods, because it seems the appropriate thing to do, despite the fact she has no idea what the Tinkerer is going on about.

"Well, using my massive knowledge combined with my unmatched inventiveness, I was able to perform a heart implant procedure. If you were to look at his chest, you would see the fresh stitches!"

"Oh, my!" Malice exclaims. "I would have just used Alice's card."

"Yes, well, that wasn't available. And besides, I rather prefer to be challenged. Using a simple card is, well, it's like cheating."

"If you say so. So do I get to use the Vorpal Fist to rip out his heart?"

"Perhaps. I thought it would be fun to make a bit of a game of it. A bit of a challenge."

Malice sighs. "I apparently don't enjoy challenges as much as you do. Can't you just give it to me?"

The Tinkerer pouts. "Well, what would be the fun in that? No, you will play my game. The three brothers are playing a game too. They believe that you are the girl they loved. You will look and sound like her to them, and their challenge is to convince you that they love you."

"But two of them are heartless."

The Tinkerer rolls her eyes. "Yes, you grasp the obvious notions of the game. Two of them do not love you. But the brother with the heart implant does. Your challenge is to figure out which one truly loves you, within the time limit, and pluck his heart out. Do that, and the fist is yours…"

"As much as I find that thought appealing, I can't help but wonder why the brother with the heart would *want* to win the game and convince me of his love."

"Well, he tells me his heart aches and yearns. He wishes only to express to you his undying love and then to give you his heart and enter the sweet oblivion of heartlessness where he no longer feels the pain of his unrequited love for you. Those were his words, not mine. Rather poetic and tragic, don't you think?"

Malice huffs. "More like pathetic. Why anyone would *want* a heart is beyond me." But in actuality she is intrigued by the concept. *What is it like to feel love?*

The Tinkerer fixes her with an appraising one-eyed-squint. "It has its perks. You might try it sometime."

Malice feels uncomfortable and changes the subject. "So what's in it for the other two boys—why are they trying to woo?"

The Tinkerer says, "I have promised them prizes if they convince you. Now, we've wasted enough time. Poor Alice is awaiting her turn. So here we go. I control each boy's senses. They cannot see or hear what the other brothers say. They have each prepared a short speech. You are to ask of each of them, 'If we were together, how would I know you love me?'"

Malice crosses her arms and says, "And if I don't?"

"Arggh! Please don't be difficult. Just do it, okay?!"

"Fine."

"Jolly good. Now, afterward, you shall make your choice as to who you think truly loves you, don the Vorpal Fist and see if it works."

Malice nods vacantly. *Which of them loves me? Nobody loves me for real. I wonder, what is it like?*

The Tinkerer interrupts her thoughts. "Ready?"

Malice nods. "Quite. Let's get on with it. I want to rip one of these cute boy's heart out. Oh, but I should make myself presentable." She struggles a few moments taking her mask off.

The Cat is laughing to mock her. He had recently given her claw scratches on her face, going from her temple to across her eyes. Of course, Malice can't tell how bad they look because she has no reflection in mirrors.

Malice says, "Will he mind the scratches? Will he still love me?"

"Um, they won't see your face. You'll look like the other girl, remember?"

Malice sighs. "He won't love me for who I really am."

"Absolutely not. So let's meet our first contestant, Brother A!" She points at the back of one of the boys.

Music plays, and his eyes widen. With a thick German accent, he says, "Girl, I've missed you! Wow, you're so pretty!"

"Thank you."

To Malice, the Tinkerer says, "Now say your line sweety."

Malice clears her throat, says, "If we were together, how would I know you love me?"

He bites his lip seductively and begins gesturing. "Girl, listen up, if we were together, I'd buy so many things for you, whatever you want, baby. You like gold? Or silver? Whatever you want. Diamonds. Rubies. I'll get it all for you."

Malice's face lights up in delight at the thought of it. "Ooh! That sounds wonderful."

"Time's up," the Tinkerer says, pressing a button, and the brother looks about, says something but is muted. "Next contestant, Brother B," the Tinkerer says. Presses a button.

The second boy looks at her. He, too, has a German accent as he says, "Hello again, darling. Oh, I've missed you so!" He begins to cry.

Did he rub something in his eyes to make himself cry? Or maybe he's the one with the heart! Or, is it a trick?

Malice says, "If we were together, how would I know you love me?"

"Because I would make time to spend with you, listen to you and care for you as best I could. Do my best to be respectful—wouldn't yell, and stuff like that."

What a sap.

"Time's up," adds the Tinkerer and with the press of a button, he goes silent.

"Thank goodness for that," Malice says. "Why would anyone reveal themselves to be so weak? Unless…he must have been really trying to trick me."

The Tinkerer says, "Brother C!" Press of button.

This guy says, "Hey you sexy thing."

Malice giggles, but then feels offended, pressing her hand to her chest in shock. "I'm 13."

The guy says, "Huh?" Now he smirks. "Not the last time I checked."

The Tinkerer uses one of her virtual reality tricks to whisper in Malice's ear, "He sees you as an 18-year-old."

"Oh," Malice says, feeling a little embarrassed. She knows the clock is still ticking, so she says, "If we were together, how would I know you love me?"

He sends her an air kiss and with smoldering eyes, says, "Girl, if you were mine, you'd see how jealous I'd get. I wouldn't be able to *stand* the thought of guys looking at how hot you are, wanting to *be* with you." He grimaces. "Why, I'd fight any guy who tried to come on to you, because I'd want you to be mine forever. That's how you'd know I love you."

"Well, I hope you mean it."

The guy nods and pounds his fist in his hand and speaks, but his volume has been cut off. But from reading his lips he's saying something about beating guys up who look at her.

The Tinkerer says, "Make your choice. You've got twenty seconds."

Malice's mind races as she thinks. The choice is obvious. Since she's heartless, she doesn't really understand love—she's never felt it and doesn't know why anyone would ever feel it for someone. But loving some*one* is like *really* liking some*thing*. And just as when you really like something, you don't want anyone else to use it.

"I choose Brother C." She grins and punches the air and makes a confident face. *I so* nailed this one.

"Is that your final answer?"

"Yeah, duh, it's a no brainer."

"Okay." She presses a button on the remote and says, "Contestants, she has chosen Brother C. What do you think of that, Brother A?"

"I'll give you a diamond ring if you change your mind."

"Brother B?" says the Tinkerer.

"I forgive you."

The Tinkerer mutes them again, and says, "Now bachelorette, I give you one last chance to change your choice."

"No can do, Tinkerer-Winkerer. You're trying to trick me. The choice is obvious."

The Tinkerer arches a brow. "Oh? I'm intrigued. Why do you say that?"

"Because Brother A was obviously trying to appeal to my greed and bribe me, while Brother B was just trying to appear meek and sappy to appeal to my desire to dominate others. But only Brother C expressed what love really is. It's like a form of ownership so strong that you don't want to share someone with anyone else, right?…isn't it?" She's starting to doubt herself a little. Maybe she doesn't know what love is at all.

The Tinkerer shrugs. "Final answer?"

To heck with it. Malice nods. "Final answer."

"Very well, then, Miss. I ask you to…don the Vorpal Fist!"

So Malice reaches and picks it up and slips it on her right hand. She tries to fit her fingers inside.

"Do you feel anything?" the Tinkerer asks.

As Malice struggles, she says, "What do you mean? It's a little big for me. I feel the metal insides. No inner padding?"

"No, I mean. You feel no tingling, or energy or anything? Feel like it's taking over you, hear whispers telling you to do things? Anything like that?"

"Nope, no, nothing like that. In fact, I think this thing might slide off my hand if I'm not careful." She lifts the gauntlet and crinkles her fingers to form a fist. She looks at it. "It's not even glowing or making buzzing sounds or anything. Are you sure this thing is magic?"

"How curious. Well, it's supposed to be magic. Of course, I haven't seen it in use. But let's try it out on your choice, shall we?"

Malice nods. "Let's."

"Brother C…prepare yourself…for the Vorpal Fist!" She presses a button and nods to Malice.

Malice steps toward him. "Um, prepare yourself…to be…disheartened…!" The contestant just sits there nodding meekly, meeting her eyes.

Malice lifts the Vorpal Fist and takes a step toward him. *Ack. This thing is heavy.* She punches with a medium amount of effort at his chest, and the guy just sits there with a neutral expression.

The fist strikes his chest with a soft thud, and he is knocked back a little bit, but remains seated. He smirks.

A tuba sound of failure issues forth, "Buh buh buh buhhhh…"

The Tinkerer says, "Oh, I'm so sorry, but you made the wrong choice. The correct answer was Brother B. That's Brother *B...*"

Malice scowls. "What? Number B? But he's a weakling!"

"Maybe that's what love is, a willingness to be weak in the eyes of someone else."

Malice is overwhelmed. She doesn't understand that at all. "What?" she says helplessly.

Brother C says, "So I won, right? I get my prize!"

"Yes, yes. Hold your horses. Stay on the line." She presses a button. "Now Miss Malice, I admit, I thought that the Vorpal Fist might not even work for a heartless being like yourself. I shall have to conduct more experiments, but I theorize it may only be used by someone with a blackened heart, not someone entirely *missing* one, like yourself."

Malice feels strangely ashamed. "Well, I can't help it, I was made this way."

"Yes, well in any case, it all worked out. You failed, so please toss the Vorpal Fist over the force field wall. I shall temporarily turn off the ceiling force field." She presses a button.

Malice hugs the oversized fist to her chest. "And if I shan't?!"

"Look, you're not in charge here. You lost, so you give the fist back. Simple. I have ways of making you comply."

Malice thinks upon that for a moment, before saying, "Fine." She flings the Vorpal Fist with rude abandon, and it lands next to the Tinkerer, almost striking her and causing her to flinch.

The Tinkerer scowls. "Hey, careful! You almost interrupted the laser!"

"I should work on my aim."

"Your turn is over." And with the press of a button she disappears, and not only that, but the three brothers and the pub-inside-a square disappear, leaving Malice inside a plain, black square labeled "Grimm Game", sullenly awaiting her next turn.

The Groundhog

Alice rolls the dice again. "Another snake eyes!" she says with a scowl. "How boring." Alice jumps on Tea Party, takes a right turn and lands on a black square labeled, "Groundhog". Just as before, the square expands and outlines of things appear without colour.

Alice sees the form of the Groundhog being outlined—he seems to be poking his head through something. Next to him is the outline of a little girl. The colors begin to fill in and the details become clearer. The Tinkerer and crew are watching on Alice's right, outside the 15 by 15 foot square.

Alice is shrieking and pressing her hands to the sides of her face as she finally makes everything out. The Groundhog is facing her with his head stuck in a guillotine, and that little girl next to him… Alice points. "That's me!"

"Yes, well it is a replica of you. One of my inventions."

"A facsimile?"

"Well, it's the actual facsimile. I mean, it's not virtual reality."

At this point, the Groundhog screams, "Let me go, please!? I'll do anything you want."

The girl is wearing a long-sleeved leotard. On the ground in front of her are written the words, "A.L.I.C.E Assault Unit". The girl looks exactly like Alice in a leotard.

The Alice replica remains perfectly still with a blank expression on her face. Everything inside the square has filled in now—it looks like the Queen of Heart's execution area, or at least a square of it.

The Tinkerer holds up a finger. "Excuse me." She presses a button on the remote and the Groundhog continues screaming and sobbing silently. "Had to mute him," she explains.

Now the Cat interrupts, "Does the replica have brains too? I should like to see her blow them out."

The Tinkerer seems irked. "You too." She presses a button, and the Cat continues speaking but can't be heard.

The Tinkerer says, "I see it was a mistake to turn his volume back on in the first place. Now where were we? Oh yes, she's one of my inventions, and I hope to create many more. She is a weapon, an A.L.I.C.E. tactical assault unit. It's a machine called an automaton that looks just like you, a sweet innocent girl, but as we both know, looks can be deceiving. For even the sweetest pussy cats..." Now she calls out to the automaton, "A.L.I.C.E., extend!" From the knuckles of the automaton's hands extend 3-foot-long metal claws. "can scratch your eyes out," the Tinkerer finishes. The automaton retracts her claws just as suddenly as she extended them.

"Kitty has claws," Alice says in wonder.

"Yes, the perfect spy or assassin. Sugar and spice on the outside, arsenic on the inside. Poke her dimples and pull back a stub, hug her, and expect to see your entrails unrolling onto the floor. And her claws aren't even the best part. Those are just her hands. And yet..."

Alice is fully aware that the conversation is being led by the Tinkerer, but she does as expected and asks, "And yet what?"

"And yet I found the project unchallenging. Unfulfilling. Anyone can create a super weapon, but how many can create an automaton that *feels,* that *loves.* It's quite an interesting challenge, isn't it?"

"Yes, quite." Alice arches a brow, and peers at the automaton A.L.I.C.E., who still hasn't moved this whole time, beyond extending her claws, that is.

"That's why I call her the 'intimacy-capable entity'. It's in the acronym."

"What's the acronym stand for?"

"I thought you'd never ask. I couldn't decide on one acronym, but I settled for just two. So it stands for both,

'Automated Little-girl Imitation Combat Engager' and 'Automated Little-girl Intimacy-Capable Entity'."

"I'm intrigued. Does she kill with kindness?"

"No, she's a killing machine of the vicious sort, much like yourself.

Alice feels an unexpected twinge of regret. She thought her heart had turned all black and remorseless. So why is she feeling a weak emotion like regret?

The Tinkerer continues, "However, I hopefully have come up with the fix to make her be much more—a companion, capable of intimacy and kindness. So she *nurtures* with kindness, at least that's the idea."

Alice feels repulsed by those words. "I'm confused. You made her able to play nice, for what reason?"

The Tinkerer scrunches her forehead up in a wrinkly mush of surprise. "Why, for the challenge of course. It would be a feat only capable of being performed by a true genius. Me." She points at herself.

"So, I'm confused. Is my challenge to fight her or have some giggling cuddle fest with her?"

"Neither. I have a bit more explaining to do before I reveal your tasks."

Alice sighs. "Well you're quite good at creating suspense, that's for certain."

She grins. "Thank you. Now, I designed the A.L.I.C.E. unit to be a companion, fully loyal to her owner. She will defend her owner at all costs. She is literally, a killing machine. Creating a killing machine whose sole nature is to kill and destroy was the easy part. I wanted to see if I could make her act in a way that was, in a sense, against her nature. As she stands there before you, unblinkily by the way—she has no need to blink. As she stands there, do you see what she is missing?"

Alice peers at the machine but sees two arms and legs and nothing missing. In fact the machine looks just like Alice herself, or Malice, absent the slashes on her face. A part of her even fears the "machine" is actually just Malice standing very still. "I see nothing missing. Perhaps something inside? Is she heartless as well?" Like so many of the creatures in Wonderland, she is implying.

"Ah, yes! You've got it! She has no heart. But… I designed one for her. I installed it with a kindness subroutine utilizing biomimetic algorithms. I hope that it can make her care, and even, I dare but hope…love."

"Darest thou?!"

"I do." The Tinkerer nods.

"I'll go rhymin's?"

"No no, algorithms, they're like mathematically based computer programs used to solve problems, or make decisions. Savvy?"

"Maths?"

The Tinkerer rolls her eyes.

Suddenly the realization comes to Alice, so she exclaims, "The Ticktock Heart!"

"That's right. Install the heart and she will become so much more than a simple killing machine. She could well become a kind, gentle, compassionate being, capable of love." Her eyes go wide with wonder as she contemplates that.

"But I thought you made the Ticktock Heart for living breathing creatures who are missing a heart."

"Yes, well theoretically, a living being can use it, but the results are unpredictable. As I often say, biological systems are so messy and unpredictable. Yes, a living thing could use the heart, but I originally designed it for the A.L.I.C.E. unit."

"So you want me to put the Ticktock Heart inside the A.L.I.C.E. unit?"

She lifts her index finger in the air. "Ah, ah…therein lies the challenge I present to you. You must make a choice. A most curious choice."

"A choice!" Alice exclaims. She can't think of anything more intelligent to say.

"Yes, this is the challenge of the square, that I present to you. You have two choices. Either you decide to allow the guillotine to fall and slice off the head of this most loathsome rodent, the Groundhog." She waves a hand at him. "I've heard you two have a history. A most bile-inducing history. Well, here's your chance…behead him and you shall keep the Ticktock Heart as your own."

"And the other choice?"

"Yes, the other choice. Or…you may decide to give up the Ticktock Heart, and install it into the A.L.I.C.E. unit's leotard sleeve, at which point she will become activated and become your companion. Of course, by deciding that, you will spare the Groundhog's life. And put away all notions of having *her* exterminate the Groundhog after activating her—I'm not that daft. No, if you activate the unit, the Groundhog shall live."

Alice says, "Well it seems quite a simple matter, doesn't it? I behead the rodent, and get my revenge and keep the Ticktock Heart to boot."

The Tinkerer eyes her with a creepy sort of half grin. "Perhaps it might be simple to someone with a pure, cruel black heart. But think upon this…perhaps the Groundhog is not all bad. Does he truly deserve to die? And what of the machine? Does it deserve to go on existing heartlessly when it could have the chance to feel, to love? Is it really such a simple choice?"

"What if I choose to do neither?"

"Then I shall execute the Groundhog on your behalf. And I would ask you to give up the heart."

Alice grinds her teeth. She is quite perturbed by the Tinkerer's controlling nature.

The Cheshire Cat yells, "Choose to kill the rat! I want to see his head roll!" The Tinkerer must have turned his volume back on at some point without Alice realizing.

The Tinkerer grins at his words, taking it with uncharacteristic good humor. She says, "Ah, mulling it over I see!"

Yes, I am. But why? The obvious choice is to kill the Groundhog. That choice is true to my blackhearted nature.

The Tinkerer seems to be pondering Alice. "Are you having doubts? I find that quite interesting. Would you like to speak to the Groundhog? Perhaps you'd enjoy hearing him beg for his life."

A part of her would very much like to hear some begging and pleading and whimpering. But there is a small niggling part of her that is not looking forward to it. She swallows, now nods. "Okay."

"Ah, splendid," says the Tinkerer, before pressing the button on the remote.

Just like before, with the Jabberwock, it takes a few moments for the Groundhog to come around. His eyes widen and he tries to look around, but his neck is restrained by the guillotine. It doesn't seem like he can see the automaton A.L.I.C.E. or the Tinkerer and others. But he's facing Alice. He squints his eyes, says, "Queen Malice?"

Alice replies, "No, it's Alice."

In his American accent, the Groundhog says, "Alice! Look, ya gotta help me get up out of this guillotine! I don't wanna die. Please!"

Alice can't help but smile. She *so* loves the feeling of power. "I have a choice of whether to let you live or die…"

"Oh, do please let me live! I'll be forever grateful! I'll make it up to you."

The Cheshire Cat shouts, "Your head's gonna roll!"

"Who said that?" He strains to look, but can't see very far. The Tinkerer presses a button, and the Cat shouts something but isn't heard.

Alice's fists clench at her side as she tries not to give in to her anger. "Do you remember…at your burrow. How you bit me to try to make me cry my magic tears on you?"

"Yes, I'm so sorry about that. I was afraid."

"Yeah, afraid for your life, and you wanted to save your hide at the expense of mine! You would have given me to the guards to save yourself."

"I'm so sorry. I couldn't think of a way out of it. But I wanted to save you. I would have used the power of your tears to help us both. I wanted to use them to get you out of there!" He's sniveling now.

The Cat is watching the Groundhog with a big grin, the Tinkerer looks merely intrigued, and the Red Queen is focused on her running.

Alice shouts, "Liar! You would have given me up! You deserve to die!"

"But look, we were both desperate. You abandoned *me* to save yourself too. You left me for dead. So we're even, don't you think? No hard feelings."

Alice gives up and lets the rage fully take over—she can feel the hatred beating in her black heart. "No hard feelings?" She looks around dramatically as if puzzled. "No hard feelings? *I* am more important than you. *My* life matters more than yours. That's why you deserve to die now."

The tears start flowing from his eyes as he starts blubbering. "Please! Please have mercy! I'll do anything! I don't wanna die." He breaks down into sobs.

Alice feels her grin creep harder. *I shall play with him, then tell him I will kill him anyway. Oh, I can't wait to see the look of terror in his eyes.* "I want to hear you beg for your life, and I shan't listen anymore to excuses. Tell me how wrong you were for what you did."

The Groundhog looks at the ground.

"No," Alice corrects, "look at me." Their eyes lock. Coldly, calmly, Alice says, "Tell me."

He looks into her eyes, his lips trembling. "Please, I beg of you. Have mercy! I was wrong for what I did. I was a coward. And I never should have bit you and for that I am terribly terribly sorry. You're right. My life is worth so much less than yours. You are great, the greatest queen ever, and I am a piece of flotsam who's not worthy of kissing your feet. I am truly sorry for my loathesome actions. I'll do anything you ask, just please please let me live." His voice takes on a high-pitched whine. "Pleaaase?!" He sobs. "I'm so sorry. So, so sorry."

Alice nods at him slowly, with a firm mouth as if weighing his words.

Oh, this shall be marvelously wicked. A few more nods to keep his hopes up, then I shall dig in the screws and tell him I will just let him die after all. I wonder if he'll scream out, or perhaps cry all the more—he does seem to cry quite a bit. I thought Americans were supposed to be rough and tough cowboys. Perhaps he'll curse me with his last dying breath, before his words shall be cut short by the guillotine blade. Oh, wouldn't that be wonderful? She chuckles to herself, but now, in midchuckle, an odd sensation hits her in the chest. She frowns a little, as she finally hears the misery driving the poor Groundhog's sobs. She actually feels sorry for him! And now she feels a strange twitching in her heart, as if her heartbeat is fibrillating. She presses her hand to her chest. *The Groundhog sounds truly terrified. Perhaps he has suffered enough. But no, what am I thinking? Surely I don't pity the rodent, but if I am willing to let him live, the* A.L.I.C.E. *unit shall become my companion—a spectacular weapon that will be loyal to me. And that is the real reason to spare his life. I see now that the Tinkerer has tried to trick me. She obviously wants me to choose the obvious choice of killing the Groundhog.*

She glares at the Tinkerer, and the Tinkerer smirks back.

Alice says, "I choose…" She taps her chin.

She Chooses . . .

Alice taps her chin a few seconds more. "I choose…to spare the Groundhog's life and to give my heart to the automaton."

The Groundhog exclaims, "Oh, thank you Queen Alice! Thank you so so much!"

Alice nods and grins at the Groundhog before catching herself and scowling. Her heart begins twitching for some reason.

Meanwhile, the Cheshire Cat shouts silently from behind the containment field. From reading his lips, it looks like he shouts, "Bollocks!" a few times.

And the Groundhog is blubbering, "Thank you," over and over again. The Tinkerer, looking disturbed by him, presses a remote button and the Groundhog can no longer be heard.

The Tinkerer says, "A wonderful choice."

Alice can't tell if she's being sarcastic. Indeed, Alice is not sure what choice the Tinkerer actually wanted her to make anymore. So Alice just says, "Promise me you'll keep the Groundhog alive." She doesn't know why she said it, because why should she care if the Tinkerer actually keeps that part of her promise—but it just seems to be the proper thing to do. She is distracted by a curious sensation of warmth in her chest and presses her hand to it.

The Tinkerer arches a brow at that. "Of course. I never cheat, and I always keep my promises. But I wonder why you should care so much about the Groundhog's well being. Perhaps the therapy is beginning to take effect."

"What therapy?"

"Doing kind deeds. Pray tell, you aren't actually feeling *compassion* for him?"

Alice feels overwhelming rage. "Of course not. I—" She doesn't know what she feels. "I just want to keep you honest. And I want my automated escort."

There's that smirk again. "Oh, yes, of course. Well if you want to turn the automaton on, simply insert the Ticktock Heart into the indentation on her sleeve."

Alice sneers. "Where she wears it…"

"Yes, you get it. She'll be a compassionate automaton who wears her heart on her sleeve. Inserting the heart shall activate her. I shall set her to remain loyal to you." She squeals and scrunches her shoulders. "Oh! Isn't this most exciting!"

Alice doesn't know what to think. *Is this some kind of trick? But I chose this, let's see what happens.*

She rummages in her dress pocket to pull out the gleaming metal contraption. She shoots a query at the Tinkerer. "She'll be loyal to me?"

"Absolutely, I promise," is the Tinkerer's response, and she does indeed look sincere.

Alice approaches the automaton with her Ticktock Heart in hand. She hadn't noticed the heart-shaped indentation before, but now she sees it on the automaton's shoulder. She touches the machine's arm, and it remains as still as a statue. *I say, there are entirely too many facsimiles of me about this place, aren't there?* She notices the skin of the automaton doesn't look quite like real flesh. It looks harder. *Perhaps it is made of that substance called plastic?*

The Tinkerer says, "Now, be a good girl and put the heart in. Take care to wind it first."

"Very well." She winds it before slipping the heart into the indentation.

The eyelids of the automaton slide up like a doll designed to mimic sleep when lying down, then open its eyes when held up. Like a machine, she turns her head smoothly to look at Alice. "Mommy?" she says.

Alice is at a loss for words. She looks to the Tinkerer, who explains, "She is initiating the imprint program. When she first starts, she needs to find out whom she is to serve and be loyal to. So tell her yes."

When Alice turns back to the automaton, the machine is holding her hands clasped in front of her chest and looking at her with big pleading eyes. Alice stammers out, "Yes, I am your…mommy." *More like twin sister…or is it triplet sister? There are way too many reproductions of me going around, it seems to me.*

The machine squeals in delight. "Ooh, thank you master! I shall protect you with my life, and vanquish any foe that threatens you, with my most fearsome arsenal of weaponry." She flicks her arms down and unleashes her claws.

The Tinkerer says, "Now the unit will perform a short demonstration before turning on completely. Its complex loyalty and intelligence programs will be booting up while it performs a kata for us."

"Kata?" Alice is distracted as the automaton quickly crouches down with her feet set wide apart, now looks around.

"Yes, it is like a dance sort of—it's meant to illustrate martial arts. It's used in karate."

"What is that?"

"It's a way of fighting, from the East, in the Asian lands. Have you never heard of it?"

The automaton starts hopping and spinning and kicking and slashing while grunting and yelling. She seems to be fighting imaginary enemies.

Alice finds it all quite dazzling, but she keeps up her conversation. "I'm from England."

"Yes, I know, but perhaps you've read of it in the adventure magazines. Ooh, there, she goes."

The automaton back flips, now does the full splits on the ground while unleashing a flurry of upward claw strokes. "Keeyah!" she yells.

She rolls on the ground, now hops into a spinning crouch kick, lands, now shoots a stream of flame from her mouth into the ground. "Ayah!" she yells,

Alice just watches, dumbfounded.

I never do anything like that. All I can do is snap necks.

The automaton stands, retracts her claws, presses her fist into the palm of her other hand, and bows at Alice.

I guess the kata is over.

The automaton announces, "I'm all booted up. I'm fully functional and willing and able to fight all your foes. Scanning." She steps in a circle. "I spy with my little eye, a giant rat, a floating cat head, a little girl, and a running queen. Tell me, master, who is friend, and who is foe?"

Alice is taken aback by the question. "I don't know... The Groundhog tried to sacrifice my life for his own, and we're not friends. So, foe, I guess?"

The assault unit's face contorts, enraged, and shrieks, "Destroy the enemy combatant!" She extends one claw and begins running toward the Groundhog, who is unaware of what's going on.

Alice wasn't really expecting this reaction. All she knows is that she was asked a question that she attempted to answer with consideration and honesty.

The extended shriek of the robot is piercing the air as her arm is extended back in anticipation of piercing the Groundhog, but just as the A.L.I.C.E. unit is about to slice him, he vanishes, and the automaton grinds to a halt, stands up straight and proclaims, "The threat has vanished, master." Her claw retracts and she bows.

Alice looks to the Tinkerer, who says, "Now why did you go and tell her that?"

The Cheshire Cat says, "Aw, I wanted to see some bloodshed!"

I guess at some point, she turned his volume back on.

And meanwhile the assault unit turns to peer at the Tinkerer and companions.

The Tinkerer continues. "You chose to spare the Groundhog, remember? So I had to remove him from our virtual perception in order to save his furry hide, speaking of which, I wonder if he'd make a good fur coat. Hmmm…" She's lost in thought.

The automaton says, "Who are those three? Be they friend or foe?"

Alice mulls it over. *I wonder if I should make that device attack the Tinkerer? Would she be powerful enough to go through the force field or smart enough to get past it somehow? If indeed it is such a wonderful weapon, it just might. But do I want to risk it?*

"Master?" the A.L.I.C.E. unit says.

But Alice is still mulling, and the answer comes from the Tinkerer. "I'm the Tinkerer. I created you. And this is the Cheshire Cat, and the Red Queen."

The assault unit curtsies. "Well first of all, thank you for creating me. I find it most lovely to be in existence."

"You're quite welcome," says the Tinkerer.

"And second," says the automaton, "are you my master's friend or foe?"

Alice chooses not to speak, but watches on with one raised eyebrow.

The Tinkerer thinks for a few seconds. "It's complicated. We have a bit of a...rivalry."

Alice huffs. "Rivalry?!"

The Tinkerer responds, "Yes, like a sibling rivalry, yeah? Love and hate mixed, right?"

Alice shakes her head slowly with her lips jutted out.

"Oh, lighten up a bit. Perhaps you'd like to try the unit's cuddle function. Might make you feel better."

The automaton looks slowly back and forth between them with an oddly calm expression as if assessing the situation.

The Tinkerer says, "You can cuddle, right? I mean, your kindness subroutines are functioning properly, right, A.L.I.C.E. unit?"

"Yes, I am fully capable of initiating and maintaining cuddling, in accordance with my kindness subroutine."

"Excellent. I am so proud of what I did in creating you."

The unit nods.

"I've a question," Alice says.

The Tinkerer replies, "Yes?"

"You wouldn't have a button on that remote that turns the unit off or changes her loyalty or anything like that?"

The Tinkerer looks offended. "Why of course not, that wouldn't be proper. The unit is designed to be undyingly loyal. Why, if I had a button, that would be like cheating don't you think? And I *don't* cheat. I have no control of her at this point."

Alice nods. "Mmmhmmm." *The Tinkerer has a strange sense of honour and honesty. I don't know why she does, but I will put it to good use.* "So I've decided," Alice says.

"Pardon?" says the Tinkerer.

Alice raises her arm and points at the Tinkerer and proclaims, "She is my foe! Attack attack attack!"

The assault unit leaps into action, extends her claws, and runs at the Tinkerer while issuing an ear-splitting shriek.

But now a couple feet away from the Tinkerer, she slams into the invisible force field which flashes green as the unit's head lurches back and with a loud cracking sound she's bounced backward onto her bottom.

"Wait, stop!" the Tinkerer shouts.

Alice shouts, "It's a force field. An invisible barrier. Try to cut through it and use your dragon fire!"

The automaton obeys without hesitation, slashing at the force field with her claws, now shooting forth flames. The flames, oddly, seem to pass through the field—they almost reach the Tinkerer, who flinches. But the unit can't cut through the barrier, yet continues trying.

The Tinkerer, with a bit of alarm says, "I cannot recommend this."

Ah, I heard that alarm in your voice, brat! Perhaps you are afraid for some reason?

The automaton kicks at the field and continues slashing, causing a ruckus of clanking sounds.

"Harder!" Alice shouts. "Use your fists! Hit it as hard as you can!"

The Tinkerer, again looking alarmed says, "Oh, dear! That is not—"

The automaton retracts her claws, draws her arm back, strikes the force field with such a loud clank that her arm is torn from her body, ripped at the shoulder which shoots sparks. The arm flings away.

"—advised," the Tinkerer completes her sentence.

Sparks are shooting from wires in the machine's shoulder. The automaton strikes the field with her other arm and that one is ripped and flung away as well.

Alice watches in shock. The machine shoots forth a stream of flame from her mouth.

The Tinkerer begins a sentence, "Tell her—"

The unit head butts the force field so hard that her head is ripped and flung backward—it sails through the air and toward Alice, who catches it without thinking.

The Tinkerer completes her sentence, "—to stop."

The automaton's headless, armless body bursts into flames. In a daze, Alice looks down at the back of the machine's head. She turns it over, and says, "Stop?"

The Tinkerer informs, "Well, it's hardly of use *now*—her head's not on her body anymore, is it?"

The automaton's facial features are twitching and her lips are curling and grimacing. In a pleasant voice she says, "My apologies master."

Alice smiles. "Think nothing of it my dear. You tried, didn't you?" Alice hears a thud and looks up to see the flaming automaton's body has fallen into the ground. It feebly begins kicking at the force field.

The Tinkerer, meanwhile is muttering, "Oh no no no…" while biting at her nails.

When Alice looks down at the automaton head, a waft of black stinky smoke poofs into her face, making her cough. The unit's head freezes while making a goofy grimace, and stops moving.

Alice asks, "Are you okay?" but it doesn't respond. "Oh, bother." Looking down at it, she says, "Me mum would always say, 'Stop making that face, or it might freeze that way'."

She giggles, but suddenly feels bad for giggling. *I actually feel* sorry *for this machine but it's not even a real person! It's just a machine!*

The Tinkerer says, "Yes she did and in this rare instance it turned out to be true!" And now Alice hears the Tinkerer crying with her face in her hands. "My robot! My beautiful invention!"

Looking over, the body is still on fire, but no longer kicking—it's lowering and raising its legs as if trying to walk.

Look at the little pipsqueak over there, crying like she's the victim. "It's your own fault! Didn't you build into it any sense of self-preservation?"

She lifts her tear-wetted face from her hands. "Alas, no, I didn't. I gave her none at at all. She was designed to do whatever her master said, and to be willing even to destroy herself if it was ordered. I didn't realize it would take you less than five minutes to get her to do so... you...you..."

"Non-automaton? At least I have a sense of self preservation. I merely did what I could to save myself."

The Tinkerer hrmphs and crosses her arms. Turns her head and looks away with a scowl.

Alice shrugs. "Should have designed her better." She looks down at the unit's head still making that creepy goofy face. It causes her to giggle in a creeped-out fashion. "Hey." She shakes the head. "Wake up." She slaps its forehead a couple of times with her palm. No go. The thing is broken. Suddenly, she remembers the Ticktock Heart. She looks at the arm on the ground as the Tinkerer says, "I *designed* her just fine. You were the one who gave her the stupid order to hit the force field as hard as she could. The force field is stronger than some robot."

Alice shrugs absentmindedly as she squints at the formerly-right arm. Its hand is opening and closing in a slow automatic fashion. *A reflex of sorts?* And there! She sees the Ticktock Heart on the sleeve, apparently undamaged.

"I say," she says, mostly to herself. "That heart on that sleeve there." She intends to drop the useless head on the ground without looking at it, but at the last second, she thinks better of it. *I should show the automaton a little respect.* She looks at it and bends to set the head upon the ground. *Wait, what am I doing? Why would I respect a machine?* Nevertheless, she follows through, and gently sets the head on the ground.

The Tinkerer looks at the arm too. "Oh, is that thing still ticking? Seems not *all* is lost, at least."

Alice is walking toward the arm. "Well do I still get to keep it, or will you use your remote control and force field to take it from me?"

"How would I use the force field to take it? That doesn't even make sense."

Alice is standing in front of the arm now, looking down. "Hey, well I'm not the genius inventor. All I know is I won the Ticktock Heart fair and square right?"

The Tinkerer waggles her hand in the air, says, "Fine, keep it. It is quite an exquisite piece of machinery. Perhaps you can manage not to set it aflame?"

Alice grins, nods, and picks up the robot arm. "But of course, why would I do that?" She punctuates with a sickly sweet smile.

"Well at least you destroyed her on accident, so it shouldn't blacken your heart," the Tinkerer admits.

"Glad to hear it." Alice plucks the Ticktock Heart out, and tosses the arm over her shoulder. "Speaking of hearts, is it too late to take the Ticktock Heart on as my own?"

"Not at all. Having a change of heart?"

"I'm considering one…"

"But not certain."

"No, perhaps if you told me—"

"Yes, well your turn is officially over, so you shall have time to consider. Do behave yourself as I attend to Malice, won't you, love?"

"Certainly," she answers with a grin. "I have little choice, now, do I?"

"Quite right." She presses a button and the square goes black and plain with large dice on the ground. With another button press, she and her entourage all vanish.

The Flamingo

Malice rolls a 4 on the dice and hops forward on the little squares. Goes past Duchess and Cook, past Knight, takes a right, goes past Tweedles. She lands on a square labeled Flamingo. The next square over is the start square.

The Flamingo square expands to about 15 feet by 15 feet. The Tinkerer and companions are watching outside the right edge of the square. The details begin to fill in. It takes a while as she squints. She makes out the details of a large bird in front of her. Now she sees it's Morley, the flamingo poet she thought she'd killed. In fact, the last she saw him, she was just about to play croquet with his dead body, when she was called away because of a false alarm of an attack.

Morley was usually a pink Flamingo, but, *My, he's looking rather pale. In fact he's looking quite ivory. But I imagine it's merely the colours not catching up immediately in this virtual reality. He must surely turn pink within moments from now.*

But alas, now she sees, everything has filled in. She is standing in what looks like a dungeon, though there are no walls in the square. All the colours are as vibrant as real life. But the Flamingo remains as white as a ghost, in shocking contrast to the red hat with the burgundy feather in it he always wears. He is shackled to the ground with heavy chains and clasps of metal bands around his legs.

Malice grunts in disgust. "Didn't I kill you?"

The Flamingo's eyes go wide in horror and he struggles at his chains. They make clinking noises. "Oh, no!" he shouts, staring at her claw marks. "I thought you might be the other one!"

"Who, Alice? I much doubt she'd be any better. She's completely blackhearted now."

The Tinkerer chimes in, "I wouldn't be so sure of that."

They both turn their heads to look at her.

The Tinkerer says, "The Queen Alice has been committing a few kind deeds of late. You might want to give it a try sometime."

"Good deeds like what?" Malice says.

"Like sparing lives." She tilts her head at the Flamingo, who makes a whimper noise that sounds a bit strangled coming from his twisted neck.

Malice sneers. "Well, to me, *kind* is a four letter word. And if there's one thing I despise, it's characters who *won't stay* dead after I've gone through the trouble of killing them." And here she makes a mocking mimic of the Tinkerer's head tilt.

The Flamingo, who has turned to look at Malice, makes a sound something like, "wauhhh!" as his eyes go wide.

"Perhaps," Malice says, "I will try to get it right next time…" She glares at the Flamingo, who starts snuffling quietly. He refuses to look at her, staring at the ground.

The Tinkerer sounds unimpressed. "Well, if you shan't commit acts of kindness on your own, I shall simply force you to. Kind of like with Alice. See, I run this show, this game. So I forbid you to kill, or harm—"

Malice interrupts, "How about maim?"

"How about scratch the eyes out of?" adds the Cat.

"…or maim or scratch eyes out of…the Flamingo." The words cause him to lift his head again.

Malice says, "Or what?"

"Or you will forfeit your turn and have no chance to win the prize."

"I don't think I much like your game. It seems rigged. And you're a cheat."

"Oh no, I may make the rules, but I assure you I don't break them. Without question. Since we needn't discuss that further, I shall now cleverly inform you that there is another reason you shan't kill the Flamingo a second time."

"That being?"

The Tinkerer pauses for dramatic effect. "You never killed him in the first place. I rescued him."

Malice sneers. "Yes, how very clever of you."

"Thank you. You see, after his neck was sliced, I was immediately alerted. My quick actions saved his life. I contrived a diversion to get you away from Morley, then using cutting edge medical procedures, I performed microsurgery on his neck, sealing the veins and arteries again. I gave him a blood transfusion to replace his lost blood. And he recovered."

The Flamingo turns to her, says, "I thank you for that."

The Tinkerer flaps her hand in the air. "You've thanked me enough. I'm more interested now in the task at hand, which is the game."

Malice is feeling rather irritable. She says, "Yes? Well get on with it, then!"

"Very well. I present to you a challenge. A riddle. If you figure it out, and act on it, you will be presented with the prize."

"What prize?"

"You shall see, or mayhaps, won't. It depends on how well you perform, I suppose. In either case, it's best not to pout, and play along, lest you want to forfeit your turn that is..." She raises an eyebrow quizzically.

"Fine, then, let's hear the riddle."

The Tinkerer nods to the Flamingo. The Flamingo looks at Malice. He clears his long throat, now recites,

There's those who change hues from the weather,
And yes, I am pale, you must think.
But *my* kind change hues from a feather,
So I ask you, please blank blank blank blank.

To laugh at what's truly a bother,
Won't require one talk to a shrink,
When this torment's brought on by another,
So I ask you, please, blank blank blank blank.

The bird nods to indicate he's done.

The Tinkerer explains, "Your task is to figure out the parts of the poem that has been left out, and to act on it. I'll give you five minutes." She gestures at Malice to proceed.

Malice says, "Well, if it's a proper poem, it must rhyme…what rhymes with think and shrink? Stink? No, pink, of course. You're a pink flamingo, or you usually are. You're looking rather pale of late, though. Your poem mentions that. 'Those who change hues from the weather…'That's a reference to browning from the sun. Am I to make you pink again, somehow?"

The bird won't meet her eyes.

"He can't answer you," the Tinkerer explains.

Malice mutters, "I figured as much. Very well…the poem says you change hues from a feather. What does that mean? Hmmm. I'm stumped. Perhaps the second verse will be of help."

Malice taps her chin. "Hmmm. The 'laugh at what's truly a bother' part… Is that like deriving pleasure from pain that your poet Swinburne enjoys?" They don't respond to her question. "Hmm, the poem says such a practice won't require one talk to a shrink when the torment's brought on by another. What does that mean? It's not crazy to laugh at torment so long as it's done by another? But that *does* seem quite mad! Only a crazy person would do that, I should think. And what's that got to do with a feather?"

She thinks for a few moments.

Feather. Laughing. Feather…

"Ah! Tickling! When one's tickled, one laughs, but it's a bother, and one can't tickle oneself, so it's a 'torment brought on by another'. Oh! And now I believe I have the missing words! 'Tickle me pink!' That's what you want me to do! With a feather?" She points at the feather in the Flamingo's hat. "With that feather! Am I right?"

The Flamingo nods.

The Tinkerer says, "Excellent. You figured it out. Now you need only act on it to pass. You have about three minutes left."

"Bah. The idea of making that wretched bird laugh turns my stomach. He'd enjoy it too much—I can't do it."

"He'd enjoy it at first like all tickling, but after a while he'd be bothered."

"Still doesn't seem proper. It'd be like playing with him, rather than killing him." She crosses her arms.

"Well then, you won't get the prize. You're running out of time. Also, I warn you again, don't tickle him to death. It's a feather from the nest of a tickle monster—it's lethal if overused."

"I shan't." Malice crosses her arms tighter and raises her nose in the air. But a part of her is thinking that she wants to win a prize.

The Tinkerer, watching says, "You're torn. I can tell. What will you decide?"

This game is rigged, but perhaps it's best I play along. I may need the prize to win, and winning is the most important thing. After all, the tickling will become a torment after a while. I could even tickle him to death! But, no I mustn't do that. He must live. Of course, I could always kill him later.

"I'll do it," Malice says as she plucks the feather from the hat.

"Ah, interesting," says the Tinkerer. "I wonder what effect it will have on you."

The bird says, "Thanks ahead of time for doing this for me. If I go too long between sessions, I turn pale, and of course, I can't tickle myself."

Malice grunts at that. She kneels and pulls one of his legs up and begins tickling under his foot with the feather.

The Flamingo begins to giggle. He tries to pull his foot away, but Malice holds it firm. The chains clink, keeping him in place. He laughs as if he's heard the funniest joke in the world. "Ahh hah hah! Stop, stop!" Malice has to focus on moving the feather properly to maximize tickle-ability, but she takes a quick glance at the Flamingo. His body is now a slightly-reddish white. The Flamingo keeps on laughing loudly but now he has to force himself to stop to take gasps of breath. "Ah ha! Please stop!" More tickling. The Flamingo's skin turns slightly more pink. The Flamingo is laughing and gasping for breath. Malice notices a tear land in the dirt beside her. "Please! Stop! It's not funny anymore!" (Gasp for breath.)

A grin creeps up the side of Malice's face. "Starting to hurt, is it? Good. I'm starting to enjoy this!"

He's wheezing and laughing, tears streaming down his face. "Please! It hurts so much! Please stop." He continues laughing but the laughter sounds painful. "Ow. Ow." He's now a light pink, but Malice won't stop now, at least not until he turns his regular shade of bright pink.

"Perhaps," she says, while wavering the feather, "I shall tickle you to death! I would so much more enjoy that than stopping."

"No, please! Ha ha ha! I beg of you, please stop. Pain…Terrible! Ah ha ha!"

"Well, at least I'm glad to know I'm no longer being kind. I daresay, I'm tormenting you."

A few tears plop onto her shoulder from above. She crinkles her eyes as she inspects the Flamingo—he's almost just as pink as she's used to seeing him.

I should stop soon if I am to win the prize.

And she feels a war erupt inside of her, as if there are two parts of her fighting each other.

No! I shan't stop! To hell with this game! I shall make sure to kill him right and proper this time. Nobody escapes from death from me and lives to tell about it!

But, no! I have to stop if I want the prize. I am the most important thing, and I must win this game if I am to conquer everyone else. So, for the sake of winning, I must stop!

No! The game is rigged! Kill the Flamingo! Don't be a pawn in the stupid Tinkerer's stupid game!

But if I do that, I will surely lose, I'll be doomed.

Screw it. Tickle him to death! Get your revenge!

Malice shouts, "No!"

She takes her right hand off the Flamingo's leg and slaps herself loud and hard across her own cheek. "I must save myself!" Her left hand is still wiggling the feather. Her right hand pushes her left hand away, quickly yanks the feather and tosses it aside.

Malice straightens and pulls her arms close to her chest. She is shuddering and feeling sickly. She hugs herself as if wishing to comfort herself.

"Oh, thank you, thank you. Thank you," the pathetic bird says weakly.

She wants to snap his miserable neck, to never hear his voice again. *No, don't look at him.*

She turns her back to him, stares at the ground of the dungeon, staring intensely at the shapes to distract herself.

She hears the Flamingo make a puzzled sound.

And Malice wants so much to speak, to tell him how much she would like him dead, to tell him she'll kill him if she gets a chance, but she fears if she speaks, she'll lose control.

And the Flamingo, thankfully, wisely, has chosen now to remain silent, because if he wasn't, she couldn't trust herself not to rise up, turn around and strangle him to death.

And so she stares. At the ground.

She hears the voice of the Tinkerer from her left, saying, "Well that was interesting. I was wondering which way you'd go. Heartless beings are fascinating subjects. Tell me, how does it feel to have committed an act of kindness?"

Shrug. "I did what I had to do."

"Do you wish to commit more?"

"Not really. They kind of make me sick."

"Intriguing."

Malice doesn't bother to hide her irritation. "Yes, well, I passed your little challenge. So what is my prize?"

"Ah, yes, well you have a choice of prizes. You may choose either the feather of the tickle monster, or 200 quid."

Malice feels the urge to strangle the Flamingo subside, so she stands and turns to face the Tinkerer. "Why would I want that stupid feather?"

The Tinkerer looks offended. "I'll have you know, that feather is one of the most highly prized feathers in

Wonderland, acquired from the nest of a tickle monster, a monster feared the land over for his ability to tickle anyone to death. It is the only feather powerful enough to tickle a flamingo pink. It is the only feather powerful enough to tickle someone to death."

"Bah," says Malice. "It's caused me enough trouble. I'll take the 200 quid."

Because truth be known, Malice can't be sure she could control herself if she used the feather, and if there's one thing she doesn't like, it's not being in control.

"Very well," says the Tinkerer. She presses buttons on the remote and gold coins appear at Malice's feet. "So, I hope you'll excuse me. It's now Miss Alice's turn. But I shall return shortly." She presses a button and disappears, leaving Malice staring at the Flamingo, who seems not to want to meet her gaze.

The Ticktock Heart

Alice thinks, *And so, shall I take on this mechanical Ticktock Heart on as my own? It is, I admit a pretty gleaming thing.*

She looks down and shifts it so the light sparkles off it. She feels the steady ticking beating lightly on her fingertips.

Why, imagine how it might gleam with a proper shining—

Her reverie is interrupted by a shout from the Tinkerer, thusly, "So, will you be putting that in your chest then?"

Alice lifts her gaze and turns to face the Tinkerer. She shouts, "If you would wish to goad me into it, perhaps it's best I shan't!"

"But you have so much you could gain from it."

Alice replies, "Me mum always used to say 'you don't get owt for nowt'."

"Yes, yes, both our mums used to say that, but it's an archaic saying. Not relevant. I mean, what, really have you got to lose? Other than a heart-so-black, that is?"

"I don't know! Why don't *you* tell *me?* Would a metal heart transform me into one of those artificial persons… one of those…what are they called—those automatons of which the boys like to read in their magazines?"

The Tinkerer says, "Make you like a robot? Well, in actions, perhaps. It might lessen your emotions or remove them completely."

"So why would a ticktock heart be better than a black heart, or no heart at all, for that matter?"

"Why, my dear little Alice, if you were equipped with one of them, you'd be much more like myself—intelligent, logical, mathematical. *Precise.* You must admit that with your heart-so-black, you're not very rational—why, you're driven by dark emotions!"

Alice sighs and nods. "Yes, that's true. But at least I *can* feel. I'd rather feel pain if it means I can feel *something.* Unlike Malice with her heartlessness. So this Ticktock Heart doesn't seem any better than the one I have now."

"But it is not *all* coldly analytical. I have experimented with some software for it, to mitigate its lack of emotion."

Alice says, "Mitigate?"

"Yes, you know. Ameliorate somewhat."

"Huh?"

"Fine. I've tried to counteract the cold mechanicalness of it."

Alice asks, "How so?"

The Tinkerer seems lost in thought. "I created a kind of computer program—a kindness subroutine."

Alice winces at the sudden mention of that word "kindness" in relation to the actions of a heart. She can feel her heart twitch, almost as if it seeks to escape the very concept by slamming out the back of her. But at least it's not as bad as a few days ago when her reaction would have been much stronger. *Perhaps it lessens with time?*

The Tinkerer notices her flinch and raises a brow inquisitively but she keeps talking. "Didn't have time to work on the subroutine very much. I say, why did you flinch just then?"

Alice almost snarls her words: "That word: kindness. When you talked about a heart doing that!..." She shudders, but not as strongly as she thought she would. *Maybe kindness isn't so terrible after all.*

The Tinkerer's face lights up in delight and she clasps her hands in front of herself in squealy delight. "Oh, I see! Your heart of black most true is repelled by the very *notion* of another heart committing an act of kindness!"

Alice flinches and shudders. "Yes, it would seem so."

"Oh, that will make my regimen all the more testable."

"Begging your pardon?"

"Well, since you now surely will not take on the mechanical heart, that will allow me to continue my methods on your black heart."

"What methods?" Alice asks.

"That I shall not divulge."

Alice arches a brow. "Are you trying to use reverse psychology on me? I've heard of that, you know."

"Absolutely—" She nods. "I am not." She shakes her head.

Alice eyes her suspiciously. "Fine. Then I will not be taking on your Ticktock Heart."

"Excellent. That shall prove interesting."

Alice sighs and slumps her shoulders and tries to stop trying to figure out whether the Tinkerer's psychology is reverse or straight forward.

The Tinkerer says, "My dear little Alice, how will you know unless you try?"

Alice scowls. "That's the second time you've called me 'little Alice'." She stamps her foot. "Why, *I'm* older than *you!* And as to trying the metal heart, the fact you want me to do so, so very much, makes me want to do the opposite. I fear that it will transform me into a machine, and I want to stay a real life girl! So I shall stick to the devil—the deviled heart I know, rather than the one I don't know. Or shall you force me otherwise?"

The Tinkerer shrugs. "It's your choice. Besides, you'd have to use the Thirteen of Heartless card to put the heart in, and according to the rule, you must have someone else to play the card toss game with to make the card work."

Alice says, "Yes. Quite. Now, I suppose I shall roll the dice."

"Very well," says the Tinkerer. She presses buttons.

Alice picks up the dice, and in a sudden bout of giddiness, giggles. She proclaims, "And nowwww…" She makes her voice go deeper and deeper until it's rumbling as deep as it will go and she bows forward at the same time. "I shall rolll these bonesssss." She makes her voice go deep again as she holds the s. Now she finishes off with a creaky kind of ribbit, just because it's funny.

She straightens up. "Here we go…" She rolls the dice. They tumble and stop as they hit the invisible force field in front of her.

She's rolled a 7.

Again the green-outlined square shrinks around her. She sees a path of blank hopscotch-sized black squares ahead of her.

So she hops forward and stands on the seventh square, labeled Flamingo, waiting.

The square grows. Now the details of what the Tinkerer had called the "virtual reality" begins to fill in, filling in the ground with stone while the Tinkerer and Red Queen and Cat are outside on the right, watching.

Alice gasps as she sees a girl standing next to her in front of a shackled pink Flamingo with a bandage around his long pink neck and a red hat atop his head—the feather that would usually go in it lies on the ground.

It's Morley, the flamingo poet—his eyes go comically wide. He proclaims, "Alice!"

Alice thinks, *As if I weren't aware of my own name.*

Now the girl in the cat suit to the left turns to her. As expected, it's Malice—she's taken her mask off and her healing scratches are visible.

And Malice proclaims, "Ah, Her Highness, Alice! You're slightly too late. I've already completed this square."

Malice's eyes flitter suspiciously about. Alice wonders if Malice will attack her.

Tension fills the square.

But the Tinkerer interjects to quell fears, by saying thusly: "'Tis folly to attack each other, for 'twould be quite against the rules, and I would not abide it. 'Twould be folly."

From between clenched teeth, Malice says, "So if I broke her throat?"

The Tinkerer answers, "You would forfeit the game. 'Twould be *so* not worth it."

"Stop saying 'twould," Alice mutters.

Alice had not been expecting to land on the same square as Malice. And she *especially* hadn't expected to do so without a fight ensuing.

Malice hadn't expected such, either.

Curious, they both think at the same time. Now they glare at each other.

The Cheshire Cat shouts, "I want to see a catfight! Mreow!"

Alice is looking at Malice, wondering if said catfight will erupt, but now she can't help but notice the Flamingo staring at her with a slack-jawed look of horror.

Finally, Alice can abide it no longer, so she turns to him and shouts, "What?!"

He stammers a bit, but finally speaks. "You're Alice, of the black black heart." He starts shuddering.

"You're scared of *me?* Surely you must be joshing me, for 'twas Malice who killed you." Alice realizes that she had said 'twas because the Tinkerer's 'twoulds rubbed off on her, and she's not proud of it.

The Flamingo says, "Yes, but she is merely heartless, sort of like a wild animal. She can't really be held responsible. But the blackhearted take pleasure in pain."

Alice huffs. "What? I overheard you even call Malice 'Our Lady of Pain'."

Malice, meanwhile is chuckling.

Now the Tinkerer interjects. "For some," she says, "pain *is* pleasure. At least according to my favorite poet, Algernon Swinburne."

The Flamingo rolls his eyes, says, "Not Swinburne again."

Malice says to the Tinkerer, "Now that is an intriguing concept. How can pain be pleasure? I seek to avoid pain."

The Tinkerer rubs her chin. "I've been trying to sort that out myself. It's a fascinating puzzle. A conundrum even."

Alice says, "Well, melancholy can be sweet, I've found…" But now she shakes her head. *Oh, what am I doing? Enough of this rubbish. I must win this game. And I know the way to* help *me win. I need only trick, I mean, convince Malice.* Alice says to Malice, "I have a gift for you. Something I won on a square of this game…"

"Oh? What is it?"

Alice reaches into her dress pocket and pulls it out. "A ticktock heart." The contraption gleams in the light.

The Tinkerer squeals. "Yes, it's good to share. I made that," she says, pointing.

Malice says, "Oh? Then I have no doubt it is a most marvelous intervention. So you want me to put that into my chest?"

Alice nods.

Malice says, "Why? Why didn't you use it?"

Alice thinks for a moment of what to say.

Alice is not *about* to say what she is thinking, which is that if she can convince Malice to take on the heart, the kindness subroutine in it might put Malice at a disadvantage in the game. She says instead, "I'll sell you the heart for 250 quid."

Malice says, "Ah and there we have the the real reason. Who says I want that trinkety thing, anyhow?" Malice doesn't say what she's thinking, which is that she's secretly jealous of those who have hearts, and wants to have one of her own, just for a little while, just to see what it's like.

Alice shrugs. "250 quid."

Malice says, "200."

"Deal."

So Alice hands the heart to Malice, who hands her coins to Alice.

The Tinkerer giggles. "Oh, so will you put the heart in now? I can't wait!"

They set about doing so. The Tinkerer presses a button to release the Flamingo from his chains, then they borrow the Flamingo's hat. Alice brings out the Thirteen of Heartless card and begins to play against Malice in the game of Toss the Card in the Hat, which they need to play in order to invoke the card's rule about putting hearts in or taking them out.

Within minutes, Malice is holding the glowing metal heart and pressing her hand into her chest—it feels almost as if she is pressing it into sand. She pushes it to where she feels her heart should rest—it doesn't quite feel right, so she adjusts her fist a little, now she opens her hand and feels the cold metal settle into place. She breathes a sigh of relief, now pulls her hand back out.

"You realize," the Tinkerer says to Alice, "you committed an act of kindness by giving her the heart."

Alice says, "Oh, bother," as she feels the warm feeling in her heart.

Malice, meanwhile, presses her hand against her chest and feels a grin stretch up her face as she feels it tick-

tick-ticking. She laughs and peers at her side in an exaggerated manner.

Alice says, "What's that?"

Malice jokes, "I'm a windup girl with a ticktock heart so—" Malice's eyes go into a far away stare as she freezes in place with her head still turned to her right.

Alice, who had been waiting for the end of the sentence, prods, "So?…"

But Malice doesn't respond. Inside of her is a crackling sensation, like an intense static electricity, spreading out from that tick-tick-ticking heart. Now it hits the outside of her brain. It feels as if large holes are exploding in her head, letting through…information…data…protocols. The neural feedback systems begin informing her of what is happening, in a stream of data.

The algorithms begin to reassert control of her sensorimotor functioning.

"Quick!" the Cat shouts to Alice. "Swat her head off!"

"Hush you," says the Tinkerer.

Malice straightens up into prim and proper posture. Her hands drop to her side.

She stands creepily still, all the while with that vacant expression.

Alice, meanwhile, is observing her. She notices that Malice hasn't seemed to have blinked in quite a while, unless *she managed to blink at the same time as me. And she's also breathing quite shallowly.*

Tentatively, Alice says, "Malice, are you okay?"

But Malice doesn't respond, being too busy staring straight ahead and standing rigid.

So Alice turns to the Tinkerer and says, "What's happening to her?"

The Tinkerer shrugs. "A meld of sorts. But I'm unsure of the details. It's never been done before. It's fascinating to watch."

And though none outside can see, inside of Malice the tumult continues. It feels as if telegraph switches click on in her brain as the Ticktock Heart connects with it and fills it with strange ideas Malice has never experienced before. Now she realizes what they are—algorithms and processes, organizational structuring, protocols of logic, segmentations of processing specializations…

Within the past few moments she has become a genius, she now realizes, able to calculate and analyze with the precision and logic of a machine.

My brain is smarter because of my heart. Curiouser and curiouser. I would not expect such a result but my anecdotal experience suggests that conclusion.

Malice finally moves, shifting her head slightly to examine Alice. Her movement is smooth and precise, unlike the twitchy, little girly way she used to move.

Alice stutters as she says, "Are you okay?"

Malice answers, "At this time, I am uncertain. I must further assess my state." She contemplates Alice.

The Tinkerer claps. "Oh goody, you're online! Recite pi to ten decimals."

Malice doesn't flinch or turn, just stays very still with a vacant look in her eyes as she states, "3.14159265353."

The Tinkerer, sounding offended, says, "That's eleven decimals! And the eleventh's incorrect!"

Malice says, "I know. But technically I did recite pi to ten decimals. You didn't specify *only* ten decimals be listed. A bit of a joke at your expense. I apologize!"

The Tinkerer laughs so hard her face turns red. "Ha! I've never met anyone with the same sense of humour as me! That was hilarious!"

"That's most unsettling," murmurs the Cat.

Alice and the Flamingo are watching on with their jaws dropped. The Red Queen stops running, and with a puzzled expression on her face, scratches her head, looks to Alice and shrugs. The lights dim slightly, and for a moment, things look like the inside of a room. Alice shrugs in return and the Red Queen resumes running, at which point the lights brighten again and the dungeon surroundings return.

Alice says, "So…how do you like your new heart? Feeling any…kinder?"

"No," Malice answers. "Emotions often lead to incorrect conclusions. Logic is a far better tool for decision-making and assessment, I daresay."

"I…see? Um, do you still want to kill me?" Alice is fishing around, trying to figure out if she can uncover this "kindness subroutine" the Tinkerer was talking about.

"My assessment of the desirability of your existence is incomplete."

Alice sighs. "You sound like a automaton."

The Tinkerer says, "But enough of this. Let's get on with the game! Alice, since you landed on a square that's already been solved, you get to roll again."

Alice stiffens and smooths her dress. "Quite right. Let's get on with it then."

The dice reappear, she rolls them, and they come up as 4. And so she hops off to her next square.

A Flamingo Analysis

Now that Alice and the Tinkerer have left the square, Malice contemplates the Flamingo, cocking her head slightly from side to side while the rest of her body stays still.

The Flamingo says, "My Queen?"

"Merely observing. The notion of deriving pleasure from pain that was mentioned, is a most intriguing concept. It is counterintuitive, don't you agree?"

The Flamingo appears nervous. "Yes, it's a silly notion of the likes of that balderdasher, Algernon Swinburne. A second rate poet. A 'Decadent', they call themselves, shouting fool notions of pain being pleasure in childish attempts to be outr'e."

Malice says, "And yet, I have heard tell of those who engage in such practices—the elicitation of pleasure from pain, that is. I've heard of those who derive pleasure from spanking, being bound, strangulation even." Her eyes rake over the Flamingo's long neck in her analysis.

The Flamingo gulps nervously.

Malice watches as the bump of his gulp travels down, down his long curving neck, before he says, "Yes, they say Swinburne enjoys it. But his skills as a poet are—"

"I rather like Swinburne. It is my opinion that you should too." She arches a brow.

The Flamingo says, "I do. Now that I think of it, he's rather good. I think I must have confused his name with someone else. I say, you like Swinburne yes? Remember the poem I recited to you? Of Our Lady of Pain? I find I am again inspired by his verse, altered to accommodate your current…condition. Shall I recite it to you, My Queen?"

Malice doesn't smile, or even nod—she merely says in a cold voice, "I look forward to the influx of data such an occurrence would provide."

"Um…so…yes?" the Flamingo says.

Malice blinks, but otherwise doesn't move. "Yes."

The Flamingo seems taken aback, but now he nods and clears his throat and in his best oratorical voice, recites:

Ah, beautiful girl so terrific!
Who ticks with a metallic heart.
Though thy mouth speaks with words scientific,
That perplex from your being too smart,
You're kinder than blackhearted Alice,
Who wants to bring us all pain,
Oh, joyless, robotic Queen Malice,
With logical brain.

Malice processes the poem.

She nods. "I appreciate the meter and rhyme of it. It's quite a successful poetical utterance."

"Thanks?" says the Flamingo.

"You're welcome. It is correct in its assessment that I have no interest in causing pain, for its own sake—not unless there is a logical reason to do so."

"I am so glad to hear that, My Queen."

"Yes." She cocks her head at the Flamingo, analyzing him. She moves to stand before him. "I am currently pondering what you said earlier, about pain being pleasure. I find it a perplexing concept. I require more data."

"Data, My Queen? I'm afraid I don't understand what— Ah!" At this point, the Flamingo yelps out as Malice quickly places her hand to the back of his neck and yanks him forward. Now she clamps her hands around his neck, choking him.

In a calm voice, Malice says, "I've heard some masochists enjoy being choked. Tell me, do you find this pleasurable?"

The Flamingo merely stares back with his mouth held open, his eyes starting to bulge out a little.

Malice pouts slightly. "Ah, perhaps you are unable to speak. Merely nod if you agree. Are you deriving pleasure from pain? Or perhaps a small amount of pleasure with a lot of pain? Respond."

The Flamingo shakes his head no.

"Curious. Perhaps an experience of equal parts pleasure mixed with pain?"

Again the Flamingo shakes his head, "no."

"Curiouser and curiouser. How can pleasure be derived from pain? Perhaps *more* pain is in order." She head butts the bird, issuing forth a thud sound.

The bird's eyes rolls back and his head slumps before he weakly lifts it again.

Malice asks, "Any pleasure?"

The bird doesn't even shake his head this time, just stares ahead with eyelids half closed. He looks as if he is about to fall asleep.

"Hmmm. Lack of oxygen to your brain, I suppose. By the way, I do so enjoy your poems. Come, I shall try to compose one myself…

"How can one get pleasure from pain,
When there seems to be little to gain?
By engaging in this act of strangulation,
I begin my process of computation.

How can one get pleasure from pain?
Tell me, doth *this,* your passion inflame?
I wish to quantify with clear objectivity,
This most kinky, anomalous proclivity.

I stand here quizzically pondering,
As the focus of your eyes is wandering,
Wondering, why would one want pleasure from pain?
Why paradoxically moan as opposed to complain?"

The Flamingo's eyes close and his head slumps. This time he doesn't raise it again.

A sharp shrill cry of "Malice!" causes her to turn her head. She sees the Tinkerer, who shouts, "Let go of that boy this instant!"

She shrugs and lets go of the Flamingo, who flops to the ground and lays unconscious with the side of his face resting atop Malice's foot.

The Tinkerer says, "You shan't go killing that flamingo poet boy! He's the only one around here who knows Swinburne!"

Calmly, Malice says, "But I was collecting data."

"Of?"

Malice is looking down at the Flamingo while jiggling her foot beneath his head. "Hmm?" She says as she looks up. "Oh, I was exploring the conundrum of the pleasure-from-pain principle."

"Oh! Like Swinburne."

Malice feels the Flamingo moving his head slightly on her foot. "Yes." She looks down to see the Flamingo with his eyes open and a confused expression on his face. She says, "There, you see? He's alright."

The Flamingo coughs and breathes in and out heavily.

Malice says, "Come, I shall rouse him." She jiggles her foot, the Flamingo shrieks in dismay, and the Tinkerer crosses her arms with a peeved expression.

The Tinkerer says, "If you want to know about pleasure from pain, you should read more Swinburne."

"Your point is noted. But I haven't any copies of your pet poet." She looks down at the distressed bird. Now she lifts her foot up and down, and the Flamingo's head as well. "Oh, rouse yourself, bird!" The Flamingo squawks and presses his wings to the ground in order to stand up.

Finally! Malice thinks. "Here let me help you."

"Well," says the Tinkerer, "perhaps I can lend you my copy if you lose the game and shall be staying."

Malice has lifted the bird, who now stands dizzily blinking at her. Malice says, "Your copy? You have a twin too?"

"No, no, I was referring to my book."

"Oh, yes, that would be logical."

"You should be more kind," the Tinkerer says. She presses a button on the remote.

Malice stands up rigid and states, "Kindness subroutine has been initiated." She peers into the bird's eyes and attempts the human facial expression known as a smile at him.

"Ah!" shouts the Flamingo. "Your face!"

My attempt to smile soothingly was apparently unsuccessful. Perhaps I should try this… "There there." She taps him on the head twice, hoping she's applying enough force.

"Ow! Ow!" His head is jostled downward.

The Flamingo shouts, "Enough of this!" He says to the Tinkerer, "I did my part. Now can I go?"

She answers, "Very well." She presses a button and he disappears. "I've got to get back to Alice and the Tea Party. Now Malice, please do behave yourself on your square until it's your turn, won't you?"

Malice nods. "As you wish. I shall merely be contemplating the nature of my new mental processing." She royal waves.

The Tinkerer grunts and, with the press of a button on her remote, she and the Cat and the Red Queen disappear from view.

A Cyber Tea Party

Alice hops past start—(The Tinkerer shouts, "200 quid for passing start!")—past the squares labeled Humpty and Troll's Riddle, then hops twice onto the square labeled "Tea Party" and the square expands to about 15 feet by 15 feet and the colors and shapes begin to fill in. She sees the a long table with three characters seated at it forming before her eyes. Looking down, she can now see the rest of the label on the ground—it says "A Cyber Tea Party". The coins for passing start appear at her feet and she absently picks them up.

And so she watches with dread as the characters seated at the table begin to become more distinct.

She bites her lip in worry. Who could be seated there? A bunch of corpses? Because all three of the characters usually seated at the table—the March Hare and Dormouse and Mad Hatter—recently died, though the

Hatter seemed to have recovered. *Perhaps the others have been revived as well,* now she adds, *hopefully.* Hopefully. Yes, she nods to herself, because a part of her really does feel sorry they died.

Maybe my black heart is not so black after all.

During this time she has been thinking, the images have become clear.

The tea table is made of black onyx and brass with lines of blue rippling about of like ocean waves. The ground is of pure black with a scribble of yellow as if a child had drawn a yellow crayon back and forth upon it for a few seconds before growing bored.

Seated at the table, as if seated for their afternoon spot of tea are three rather woeful looking creatures who seem to be trapped inside metal contraptions holding them in place.

She recognizes the Mad Hatter. He looks uncomfortable and perturbed, held in the metal suit that holds his arms and neck and head. The odd constrainment device holds him from the back, leaving the front of him viewable, with a few straps and buckles here and there. To the left is a large rodent—is it the Dormouse? He's also held by a metal constrainment device. She squints her eyes. No, it's not the Dormouse. She gasps. It's the Groundhog!

She looks to the Hatter's right side to see that it's not the March Hare who is sitting there with his arms awkwardly held up in front of him by metal constraint.

It's the White Rabbit, who happened to be the March Hare's nemesis.

And finally, Alice's eyes are drawn to the tabletop, where, amongst the teacups and teapot, and the pies and saucers as well, there is an odd brass replica of a large daddy long-legs spider. That had definitely not existed in the usual, real-world, or rather Wonderland-world version.

She's staring at it, trying to figure it, when the sudden voice of the Tinkerer causes her to jolt in surprise.

"I made a few changes," the Tinkerer says from the square's right edge.

Alice, feeling a bit too overwhelmed to come up with words, looks at the Tinkerer and says something akin to, "Euugh?"

To the utterance, the Tinkerer responds, "Yes, well the actual version of the tea table was rather…bland don't you think? I decided to take certain…liberties. To spruce it up, of course. Natural colors are so predictable and redundant. Why bother, I say."

Alice looks to the three seated figures at the table, who seem unaware of what's going on.

Alice says, "Very well. Speaking of differences—"

"Ah, yes, you may have noticed that they're not the original cast of characters. I admit, I had to make concessions. The Mad Hatter is the original one, because I managed to revive him. But I've had to employ stand-ins for the other two because they're deceased, you see. So playing the role of the Dormouse is the

Groundhog—they're both rodents, by my figuring. And playing the part of the March Hare is the White Rabbit."

"But they both hated each other!" Alice protests.

"Yes, they quite did. But, rabbits and hares, what's the difference? I needed someone to play the part."

Alice raises her brows and gestures with her head at the contraption holding the White Rabbit in place. "He doesn't seem so happy about it…"

"Ah, you've an astute eye! I knew it wouldn't take you long to notice! Yes, all three are quite the uncooperative sort, especially for the game I have in mind. So I fitted them all with mechanical exoskeletons that will lock them in place and force them to move as I command. The game would not work otherwise. They would have rebelled."

"What game?"

"Ah, now we come to it. The game is called Russian Roulette. Have you heard of it?" And now she points at an object resting on the table that Alice hadn't noticed before. It looks like a pistol!

"Isn't it some kind of gambling game? There's a spinning circle and a ball that lands on a number and if you picked it—"

"Ah, yes that is the regular kind of roulette. Russian roulette is similar, but morbidly different."

"Vodka!" Alice exclaims.

The Tinkerer cocks her head. "What's that?"

"I remember me mum saying the Russians drink vodka. She said it's like drinking fire."

"Ah well, we haven't any vodka, just tea. Speaking of which, why not have a seat at the table and a spot of tea? You'll get to see my marvelous inventions in motion."

Alice points. "But there's a spider! I'm deathly afraid of spiders."

"Oh, that's not a real spider, my dear. It's merely a machine. One of my inventions. It's like a little servant."

Alice sighs. "Very well." She takes a seat on one of the eerily glowing chairs.

"Now, I shall turn on the perceptions of those three so that they may enjoy their beverages. But since I can't have them squawking, I shall take measures to ensure they're silent." And with that proclamation, she presses a button on the remote.

The three characters start blinking rapidly as they stare at Alice, but their hands and bodies stay still, locked in place, as it were.

The Mad Hatter proclaims, "Alice!"

And the White Rabbit says, "This kidnapping is making me late, for an important date."

The Groundhog doesn't say anything.

"Silence!" the Tinkerer shouts while pressing a button.

The three wince and yelp unsilently one last time. The Groundhog seems to want to say something, perhaps to state that he didn't say anything, but thinks better of it.

The Tinkerer looks at Alice, says, "I've told them if they don't obey my commands, I shall shock them."

Alice notices now that all the three seated characters are trembling. The White Rabbit, she notes, looks particularly distraught, with his eyes closed and his mouth held tight and crookedly. She has no problem admitting to herself that she feels sorry for them, and doesn't feel bad for feeling sorry for them—no matter what her heart is supposed to make her feel.

She feels particularly bad for the Hatter. She looks at his deep frown. *Why do I feel this way? Maybe because he's the only human, or maybe because I've spent the most time with him, and am closest to him in a weird way.*

She sighs. *My heart be damned, but if I could set them free right now, I would.*

The Tinkerer clears her throat. "I *said*, do you care for a spot of tea?"

Alice shakes her head out of her reverie, and in a reflex of politeness, says, "Yes, please, that would be delightful. Shall I pour it myself?" she says, looking doubtfully at the locked-in-place three characters.

"Oh no!" says the Tinkerer. "You stay right there, and prepare to be amazed!"

She presses a button on the remote. The metal spider rises up upon its spindly long legs. With sounds of clicks and whirs, it slinks toward the teapot, now uses two of its arms to lift the teapot by the handle while another holds it steady. Alice is amazed by the complex movements of this machine as well as by its strength.

It's so graceful, it almost seems alive, though its movements are slower and more methodical than an actual spider would be.

The mechanical spider makes its way to the cup in front of Alice and pours steaming tea into it, stopping its pouring at the proper level.

The Tinkerer says, "Sugar?"

"Yes, one lump please."

The spider goes to the sugar bowl, retrieves a cube and slips it in her cup, grabs a spoon and places it on the table beside her cup.

"Thank you," Alice says to the spider with a bow of her head.

"It can't really hear you. It's just a machine."

As Alice stirs her tea she says, "Yes, well, in any case, it's best to maintain one's manners, don't you think?"

The Tinkerer's reply is, "As you wish."

Meanwhile, the metal spider is scurrying about the opposite side of the table, pouring tea for the other three.

I wonder how they shall manage to drink it? Alice thinks to herself.

The Tinkerer looks off to the side. "Excuse me one moment—Malice is choking the flamingo. Be right back." She presses a button and disappears from sight.

Alice patiently awaits the Tinkerer's return.

"Sorry about that," the Tinkerer says. "That's what I get for forgetting to blank everything before I leave a square. So where were we? Oh yes, sugar." She presses a button.

Alice blows upon her tea, before taking a sip. "My, this is quite good."

"Yes, well it is virtual reality tea, so only the best, I say."

Alice is watching as the mechanical spider is plopping one cube of sugar in each of the cups.

After plopping a sugar cube in the White rabbit's cup, the spider returns to its original position on the table, lowers its legs and goes still.

The White Rabbit is frowning. He says, "I would like to request a second lump of sugar, please. I like my tea very—"

"Silence!" shouts the Tinkerer, and the White Rabbit grimaces and grunts, but otherwise doesn't move.

She must have pressed that button again. I wonder if it is labeled, "shock" or somesuch.

She gestures at Alice. "Go on, enjoy."

Alice guiltily takes another sip of her own. It's really quite good. Although, it's supposedly virtually good, so maybe it's not *really* good, maybe it's only *virtually* good.

Best not to think too much on it, perhaps.

Alice smacks her lips and tips her cup at the Tinkerer. "It's an exquisite blend, my dear."

The Tinkerer bows slightly. "Why thank you dear. I designed it myself, within the virtual reality parameters. At first it wasn't quite to my standard but I tweaked its sensory output until it was perfected. Quite proud of it, I am."

Alice takes another delightful sip and nods and hmms her agreeance.

The Tinkerer nods and hmmms back. "And now!" she announces, "Watch my exquisite machinery in action!" She presses a button and now, with whirs and clicks, the right arms of the three characters begin to move in completely synchronized motion as the rinky dink song of Pop Goes the Weasel plays, as if it were coming from a wind up jack-in-the-box toy. The arms lower in a mixture of jerky and smooth motions combined, glide out to grasp the cups at the same time. The expressions on the faces of the three seated characters look quite cringey.

Obviously they're upset to find their arms moving of a will all their own.

Their arms slowly raise in time to the song—Alice forgets herself, and out of habit, at the end of the song, she shouts along, "Pop goes the weasel!" as the hands of the three tilt back to the three's mouths. The Mad Hatter is ready with his mouth open and the tea splashes sloppily into his mouth as well as some upon his face.

The White Rabbit and Groundhog seem to be trying to turn away, with their lips held tight and so the mechanized arms only succeed in splashing the liquid across their faces.

What a waste of good tea.

The Groundhog whimpers. "Why? I'm just a groundhog."

The Mad Hatter swallows and says, "Mmmm."

The White Rabbit pouts. "I said I wanted *two* lumps."

The Tinkerer arches a harsh brow. "Two lumps on your head? It can be arranged."

And now the Mad Hatter adds, "It is most delightful. I can die now."

The Tinkerer says, "And well you might. So now I have demonstrated that I am in complete control of those three's arm movements, though not their mouths. After all, it seems you can lead a groundhog to tea, but you can't make him drink."

The Groundhog merely whimpers.

The White Rabbit mutters, "Well *I* would drink, if I had the required amount of lumps, and no, not *head* lumps." Alice imagines that if he could, he would cross his arms, but seeing as how he is mechanically constrained, he does not.

The Tinkerer says, "Yes, well now that I have demonstrated my control of your movements, that brings me to the task at hand and the challenge of this square. Now let us revisit the game of Russian Roulette."

Russian Roulette

The Tinkerer points. "You see that pistol there? It is not an inferior, old-fashioned single shot flintlock pistol, oh no. Technology progresses, and what you see is a pistol capable of holding and firing six bullets before needing to be refilled again."

Most everyone gasps, two of them exclaim, "Six?!"

"Yes, six. The gun is called a revolver, because the bullets are held in a container that revolves each time the trigger is pulled. I admit, I could have made a laser pistol, but that wouldn't have been quite the same. Not as traditional. So there is the revolver. It may only be a virtual gun, but believe me, it is quite capable of killing you *for real,* even though the creatures of Wonderland have a bad habit of coming back from the dead, though I have a hard time fathoming how one could rebound from having one's brains blown about."

At this point, the Tinkerer looks to her right to see the Cheshire Cat excitedly bouncing within his confinement. "Oh, the Cat does so much like the idea of flying brains smashing about. Good thing he's on mute, don't you think?"

Alice shrugs.

The Tinkerer says, "Well I think he's quite a sicko. Like all cats. If you died, they'd eat your face for food—they don't care. But in any case, to the matter at hand."

Alice snarls. "Yes, let's get on with it…"

"Very well. In the game of Russian roulette, there is a revolver with six chambers. Only one of them has a bullet. The player who goes first, spins the revolver, points the gun at his head and pulls the trigger. There is a one in six chance he shoots a bullet into his head, right? But in this version of the game, those are the best odds. If the gun doesn't fire, he hands it to the one on the right. The chances of the bullet firing become one in five. If it doesn't go off, so it continues, the odds getting worse and worse. Eventually, someone loses. It's an odd game, don't you think?"

"To what purpose?" Alice says.

"Well, I would think the players all hate each other and wish each other dead. There is no other use for the game. Other than for the amusement of a sadistic gamemaster that is, like me. So, in any case, the challenge of the square is to offer you a choice."

"Choice?" Alice says.

"Yes, in this square I offer you a choice to decide which of these three to go first in the game, keeping in mind that the one who goes first will have the best odds. I want to make it clear that only those three will be playing and you will be watching. Once you make your choice, you will be rewarded the Vorpal Fist, a weapon of great power."

Alice's eyes light up at the mention of weaponry. But quickly, guilt overwhelms her, which confuses her. *Why am I feeling this way? I thought I was blackhearted! Shouldn't I revel in being in control of the life and death of others? But no,* she shakes her head, *I don't feel right about this.* She actually *resents* being manipulated into choosing. "They won't stop pulling the trigger?" she whimpers.

The Tinkerer answers, "If you make the choice, eventually someone will lose."

"A sorry lot, they are. Even the White Rabbit. Such vicious things he did to me."

"So whom do you hate the least? They would go first, I should think."

Alice ponders while the three look on, imploring pity with their eyes. She has a particular fondness for the Mad Hatter. Sure he'd taken pleasure from her pain, but he'd never actually done anything terribly bad to her, and she feels guilty for snapping his neck. *So perhaps I should choose him to go first. But then again, if I choose him and he shoots himself, I shall feel terrible.*

But now she screws her mouth up in determined defiance. "And if I refuse to make the choice?"

"Well, you shan't get the Vorpal Fist, and if the game is to proceed, someone must decide and that someone would be me."

"Well, I object to the game on principle!" And now a surge of warm pride rises in her chest. "None of them deserves to die. Punished, mayhaps, but not killed. Therefore I choose for none of them to go first, and I demand that you call off this sick game!"

Alice crosses her arms and feels the warm sensation grow warmer and looks down at her chest, but it's not glowing as she expected it to. A puzzled expression crosses her face.

The Tinkerer peers at her. "My, my that's rather righteous of you. Perhaps your heart is not so black after all. But then, who are you to demand I stop? You are merely a player in my game. Perhaps you'll reconsider." She taps her chin. "But if *I* were to choose, whom would it be?"

Alice says, "I implore you. Put a stop to this. They don't deserve this." She looks at the chattering and trembling of the three and she feels pity in her heart for them.

"Now you're imploring? I think…" She rubs her chin. "If I were to choose, I would choose…the Hatter!"

"Please, I ask of you not to do this!"

"Ah the magic word. You're being more congenial." She shrugs. Pushes a button. The mechanical spider clicks and whirs into motion, picks up the pistol.

Alice watches in horror as it spins the bullet cylinder. "Please! I beg of you, stop!"

The spider places the gun in the Hatter's hand. The exoskeleton forces his fingers to hold it. The Hatter is trembling and looks horrified. He tries to put on a brave face, as he says, "Who knows, maybe I'll miss. I've only half a brain."

Alice laughs in sympathy as her eyes well with tears. She whimpers, "Please…"

The Pop Goes the Weasel song begins to play as the Hatter's mechanized arm slowly raises the gun.

"However," the Hatter continues, "half a brain is still more than the rodent there."

"Hey!" the Groundhog shouts.

Alice loses all control. "Please, I beg of you to stop it! I'll do anything you want!" The tears are streaming down her face and she's taking big gasps of air.

The Pop Goes the Weasel song continues, the arms of the machine holds the gun with the barrel pointing upward.

"Stop it?! Stop it??!" the Tinkerer says, as the arm presses the gun to the Hatter's temple—he closes his eyes and it's almost the end of the song.

"Very well," the Tinkerer says. Now she hops up and shouts along, "Pop goes the weasel!"

The Hatter winces, just as Alice herself does. Alice is hysterical now, breathing fast, her heart racing.

But there's no boom or click. The arm never pulled the trigger.

The Hatter opens one eye tentatively.

The Tinkerer meets Alice's eyes, says, "You pass."

Alice wipes her cheeks. "What?" she says as she reflexively presses her hand to her chest. Her heart is feeling warm again, but oddly good and it makes her smile.

The Hatter opens his other eye and grins, "I say, the arm has quite got the aiming part down, but is perhaps dodgy on the concept of how to work a trigger. Here's a quick instruction: pull." He chuckles.

The Tinkerer says, "Don't push your luck."

He replies, "Well if you asked me to *pull* it, I would certainly do a better job of it than this machine arm here."

The Tinkerer rolls her eyes and looks to Alice again.

"What did I pass?" Alice says.

The Tinkerer answers, "I wanted to see if you were capable of an act of kindness, whether you'd be willing to sacrifice for the sake of someone else. And you demonstrated that you are."

"Yes, that's rather strange, isn't it? I thought my heart had turned black."

"It did, but I've been working on a theory that a black heart might be able to be reversed, if that person commits acts of kindness."

"But a blackhearted person wouldn't do kind deeds in the first place."

"No, not unless they were forced or tricked…"

Alice finds herself beaming. "Why you little scamp! You made me do nice things!"

"Yes, it was an experiment."

"So am I cured then? My heart's all red?"

"No, I doubt it works that quickly. I think your heart must still be partially blackened, but given enough time and good acts, it might go all red. But it's still an experiment."

Alice nods. "Well thank you."

"No problem at all my dear. I did it merely out of intellectual curiousity."

"So you say." She winks.

The Tinkerer doesn't respond to that. She says, "So are you ready for your prize?"

"Sure. I still get it?"

"Well, yes, you made your choice, didn't you?"

She presses a button on the remote, and a circle opens in the floor in front of Alice. A pedestal slides up with a metal object on top of it.

Looking down at it, Alice sees that it is a black metallic glove adorned with sparkling red heart-shaped rubies.

"Behold!" the Tinkerer proclaims. "The Vorpal Fist!"

Alice lifts it up. "Ooh, it's pretty. Does it do anything special?"

The Tinkerer says, "The Vorpal Fist has an uncanny ability to seek out the hearts of adorers, to punch in and rip their hearts out and show it to them before they die. But it only works if the wearer has a black heart, or maybe at least a partially blackened heart. In any case, I wouldn't put it on unless you plan to use it. And also I present to you, a companion. The Mad Hatter to help you in your hunt. With him by your side, I'm sure you'll have a greater chance of finding the Snark."

Alice feels a little thrill go through her. She's always kind of had a bit of a crush on the Hatter, despite her once having snapped his neck. But she tries to hide her excitement. "Okay, if he wishes to."

The Tinkerer says, "Hatter?"

He beams his charming smile. "Oh, I'd be glad to help her find the Snark. She's gonna need it, because she'd have a hard time finding her own head if it weren't attached."

Alice frowns a little.

The Hatter says, "Oops. Just teasing a little."

Alice puts on an uncertain grin. Had the Hatter always been that, for lack of a better word, snarky? *Oh, but he's just teasing me, and he's so gosh darn cute!*

"Wow, you're annoying when you talk," the Tinkerer says. She presses a button and mutes him. "Well, pardon me, but it's Malice's turn. Oh wait, I mustn't forget to clear the square before I go!" She presses a button and she, Red Queen, Cat, and the Groundhog and White Rabbit pop out of view, leaving Alice with the Hatter seated at the table.

Alice shouts, "Hey wait, you forgot to release him!"

Alice looks at him and shrugs.

He rolls his eyes and says something that's perhaps rude, but she can't hear.

The Wingless Butterfly

Malice rolls the dice. The chance event result is 7. She passes start, at which the Tinkerer yells, "200 quid for passing start!"

She lands on a plain black square marked, "Butterfly". The square expands, and now Malice gazes in calm contemplation at the sight before her.

It takes a few moments for the details to fill in. Now she sees a large wingless butterfly floating in place, wearing some sort of fire-spewing backpack machine. The machine sways slightly while making sounds like a blowing furnace. The machine seems to be tethered by some sort of gray rope attached to a pole. The rope is obviously fire proof because it's attached to a point right behind the flames. The flying machine is straining at the rope as if trying to fly free. The insect's face is set in nauseas unease. He's wearing a monocle in one eye.

Metal arms project from the sides of the machine to two of the butterfly's arms, where there are joysticks and buttons. Malice deduces that is how the insect controls the machine.

She also notices something else most curious: a gray piece of spongy material is taped to the butterfly's side with long copper wires sticking out two ends—one end leads to the Butterfly's forehead, where it is taped there, the other end leads to the top of the machine—another piece of tape affixes it in place there.

Most curious.

From the right side of the square, the Tinkerer says, "I'm hoping you can help me with a bit of a predicament." She nods at the insect with the wide eyes who looks like a tether-ball flapping about in a fierce wind. And the bug is muttering to himself, "Whoa, whoa" and groaning most pitifully.

"Who is that?" Malice asks as she bends to pick up the quid that have appeared at her feet. The square has filled with a plain gravelly field. She sees a small black cylinder on the ground beside the coins.

"Why that is the poor little, well he *used* to be little, Wingless Butterfly. I have temporarily enlarged him using mushroom enlargement technology to aid the procedure. He's the former caterpillar who used to sit Alice on his lap and have her partake of his hookah. I was just trying to help the chap out." With her eyes she indicates the flame-spewing machine.

"He doesn't seem to be in very good control of that whatever it is machine."

The Tinkerer winces as if the words struck her. "It's *called* a jet pack, and I invented it myself."

At this moment the insect lurches sickeningly and lets loose a most lamentable yelp.

Malice smirks. "He doesn't seem to be appreciating it much."

The Tinkerer crosses her arms. "Yes, well it just has a slight design flaw. I can hardly be faulted for forgetting. I mean I have so many things on my mind. I've invented so many inventions these past few days, all of them brilliant. I am bound to forget one or two things, out of thousands of things. Thousands. Millions perhaps!"

Malice arches her brow. "What did you forget?"

"Okay, first of all, it's not a major mistake. The Butterfly *begged* me to invent something to allow him to fly after Alice cut off his wings. And I *did* that. It works even better than his old wings! Because the jet pack can fly higher, thousands of times faster—it can even break the sound barrier, did you know that?"

Malice is at a loss for words, not really knowing what that means.

So the Tinkerer explains, "At its maximum setting it can fly faster than the speed of sound! And since it runs on nuclear power, it can run for thousands of years without needing fuel."

"No coal?"

"No coal."

"Ah but you forgot to tell me what you forgot…"

The Tinkerer crosses her arms and shivers. "Okay, well my jet pack is brilliant. Much better than wings. I was simply distracted. I simply neglected to include—and I can hardly be faulted, for the invention is so brilliant, why would one even want to do so,—but I forgot the tiny matter of including a way to turn the jets off."

Malice sees the Cat chuckling silently in his containment field.

Malice laughs. "You mean to tell me there's no off switch!?"

"Regrettably, no. And his velocity is currently at its highest setting, past the sound barrier. It was quite a feat to capture him, and tether him, and enlarge him, let me tell you. By the way, it was ingenious how I managed to enlarge him."

"Do tell."

The Tinkerer tells, "I discovered that if I run a positive electrical current through a piece of his special mushroom, it temporarily enlarges things. See the copper wires? As long as electricity flows through them, the jet pack and butterfly will remain enlarged. It doesn't affect the monocle though."

Malice arches her brow. "And if the current is cut off?"

"Then the jet pack and butterfly will instantly shrink to their original size."

"How instantly?"

"Instantaneously instantly. Why?"

"Just curious. What of the monocle?"

"Oh, that won't shrink because I originally made it at the size it is now."

"Curious."

"Indeed."

Meekly, the Red Queen says, "Excuse me, I hate to interrupt."

"Yes, what is it?" the Tinkerer says.

"I was just wondering, could I possibly use one of those jet packs to, you know, get to places faster?"

The Tinkerer rolls her eyes. "You've got nowhere to go! So, no. Please go back to your running, won't you?"

The Red Queen doesn't say anything in reply. She keeps running.

The Tinkerer says, "Now where were we?"

Malice says, "We're at the point where I ask, what does all of this have to do with me?"

The Tinkerer taps her fingertips together. "And this is the part when I ask of you a favor, based upon your specialized abilities."

"Yes? Proceed with your inquiry."

"I hope you will forgive me for using the game to encourage you to do the task. I doubt you would, otherwise."

Malice shrugs. "It is logical for you to do so."

"Yes, quite. Well the challenge is this." She points to the small black cylinder on the ground. "That is a laser scalpel. It's like a razorblade, but it uses concentrated light to cut. It is ideal for surgery because its heat seals the wound to prevent bleeding and infection."

Malice says, "Intriguing." She kneels to pick up the scalpel.

"Yes it is. The suit and scalpel is not a part of the virtual reality. It is real. I made a promise to the Butterfly that I would do my best to come up with a way to allow him to fly, a way that he could control. I gave him the jet pack—my goal was to turn him into what I like to call a cyborg—his body would be melded with the machine so that he could control the jet pack with his thoughts. However, I couldn't pull that off. I gave him those joystick controls until I can figure out how he can control the machine with his mind. With the aid of the mushroom driven enlargement technology, I melded his body into the insect sized machine, but I ran into some…difficulties. Seems it was a bit harder than anticipated. I would have liked to make some alterations to fix it, but the Butterfly complained. He wants organic wings, he says, despite their inferiority."

The Tinkerer sighs. "I still feel bound by my promise. I never break a promise. The Butterfly was really quite adamant in his protestations. He's really quite an obnoxious fellow. All the jet pack needs is a few tweaks, I'm sure of it. It's a marvelous machine."

"I concur. It's a marvelous feat of engineering."

She smiles big. "Why, thank you! But does *he* appreciate it? Nooooo…I even made him a special monocle, which he didn't like either. And did I mention he's a jerk? Wants me to grow him a new hydroponic garden of live talking flowers so he can smoke their spice. He doesn't really *deserve* my technology if you ask me. So what I want, what the challenge of this square is, is to cut the Butterfly free from the jet pack, using the laser scalpel and monocle."

Malice's thought algorithms quickly assess the situation and attempt to incorporate the kindness subroutine. *The Butterfly is obnoxious, and the Tinkerer actually seems bothered by the thought of dealing with him anymore. In my analysis, she subconsciously does not want to fulfill her promise to him. Wouldn't it be an act of kindness to figure out a way that the Tinkerer can get out of her promise?*

Malice calculates the probability of success of an act of trickery to attain the incident of kindness. *Sometimes it is more kind to be deceptive.* So Malice smiles, says, "It sounds more like you wish to cut the beautiful machine away from that obnoxious insect."

The Tinkerer chuckles. "Well, I suppose that's the more accurate way of putting it! If you cut the jet pack away—"

Malice, still calculating how to lead the conversation, interrupts with a friendly, "Yes, cut the jet pack loose!"

"Ha, cut it loose! I like that!"

"It would be like the machine would be escaping a biological whiny little insect!"

"Haha! Yes, he is one. He wants to trade my marvelous machine in for meager biological wings. It will be a challenge. I will have to figure some way to spur his body to initiate new growth." She sighs. "Biological systems are so messy. Not like machines at all…"

Malice, still trying to sound chatty, concurs with an eye roll. "I hear ya sister."

The Tinkerer nods at that. "Yes, sister."

Malice, still attempting her manipulative actions, chooses distraction. "What is so special about the monocle?"

"Oh? Did I not mention? It's another of my inventions. I have altered it so that it shoots out x-rays. By peering into it while pressing a button on it, one can see *inside* objects. It will aid you in your surgical procedure. Combined with your machine-like precision, I am confident you will pass the challenge. If you pass, the scalpel and monocle are yours."

"And if I fail?"

"You forfeit both objects and your turn will be over."

"And I am to believe you?" After the distraction, challenging her, also, is part of Malice's scheme. *I have her right where I want her.*

"Yes. I do not cheat."

"And you do not break promises, so would you promise me this…"

The Tinkerer motions with her eyebrows to proceed…

"Promise me," says Malice, "that if I cut the machine free, as you put it, you'll allow me to keep the monocle and scalpel." Malice hopes the Tinkerer's subconscious desires will cause her to pass over the loophole in what she just said.

"I promise. So shall we proceed?"

Malice nods, practices her organic-looking smile. "Let's." Meanwhile she's thinking, *my little trick seems so far to have gone undetected.*

"I shall now shift the Butterfly's virtual perception so that he can see and speak with us. Oh, and one thing—don't mention the word surgery. He'll freak out. He's deathly afraid of even the *word.*" She presses a button on the remote.

During these next several seconds, the expression on the Butterfly's face shows he's intrigued, now surprised, now his eyes go wide and he looks madly about. "Alice!"

The Tinkerer says in a trying-to-calm-him voice, "You are still in the virtual reality, remember? I have just turned your sight and sound back on so you can see me, and Malice here."

"Malice?" he says.

Malice replies, "Yes, I'm Alice's twin sister, except she has a black heart, and I have *no* heart."

The Tinkerer jumps in, saying to the Butterfly, "Now you remember what we talked about earlier? Give your monocle to Malice so she can perform the um, procedure."

"Procedure?!" he shouts, sounding on the verge of an all-out panic.

The Tinkerer lifts her hands palms up and pushes at the air twice. "Now, now. She knows what she's doing—she's very precise, and it shall be over before you know it. Think of it as like you're being set free. Then you can get your biological wings you want so much. Won't that be nice?"

The Butterfly takes a deep breath and seems to calm significantly. "Yes, that sounds good. But I'm so so afraid of…I can't even say the word."

The Butterfly is terrified of surgery. Wouldn't it be an act of kindness to make it so he doesn't have to have surgery performed on him?

Malice says, "I shall set you free." And she tries out the beaming smile she's been practicing.

The jet packed butterfly smiles back.

"So give her the monocle…" the Tinkerer says.

The Butterfly snaps to attention. "Oh, yes, quite right." With one of his long insect arms, he grabs the monocle he's wearing. "Catch," he says, and tosses it to Malice, who catches it.

"Smudged a bit," she mutters. She rubs the monocle with her thigh. She holds it up and peers at it. *Ah, that's better.*

The Tinkerer says, "Quite right. So, I say now…be a good chap and try to remain still so that Malice here can do her thing and set you free."

At her self's mention, Malice grins broadly, hoping her dimples pop prominently. *I say to myself, this whole biological notion of smiling is quite simple once you get the hang of it.*

The Butterfly, with an alarmed expression, says, "I say, my girl, what's wrong with your face?"

Okay, perhaps not so much.

She makes a show of holding her hand over her forehead, now passing it over her mouth, and revealing an exaggerated frown instead. "Never mind that. I'm eager to try out this monocle. Now stay still..." She presses the button then lifts the lens to her eye.

"I'm trying! Now, mind the flames, girl."

"Yes, yes, I'm not an idiot." She has to position herself by leaning backward and stooping and looking up at the Butterfly's body. She closes one eye now to focus on what she sees. She sees a glowing green version of the Butterfly, and the shapes of his internal organs. She sees the absence of a heart in his chest and she sees how the machine melds into his flesh with several shallow rods into the sides of the Butterfly's body. "Why, how intriguing this is. I can see inside him!"

The Tinkerer says, "So now you can see better, yes?"

"Affirmative."

"So, when you cut, make sure not to get any of the machine! The flesh can heal."

In a panic, the Butterfly says, "Cut? Flesh?!" The suit warbles a little.

The Tinkerer says, "What? Forget I said that. She will—"

"Release him," Malice offers.

"Yes, release you. Think how great it will be to set you free. Close your eyes, breath. Relax."

The Butterfly does so, and his suit goes back to a steady hold. "Yes," he murmurs, "release me."

The Tinkerer peers at the Butterfly, now says, "Proceed."

Malice nods. *Curious,* she thinks to herself as she analyzes the penetration points of the jet pack's rods. She uses her analytical algorithms to calculate what incisions she would use. She has no doubt she would be able to perform them—the Ticktock Heart allows her to precisely control the movements of her body.

The Butterfly would survive and require a short period of healing to recover.

My, that was an invigorating challenge! It would have been quite an accomplishment to have gone through with it. But, I must commit my act of kindness.

Calmly, Malice three steps to the left and stands up straight. She presses the back of the laser scalpel and uses it to slice through the cord tethering the jet pack to the pole. It streaks off and smashes into the force field with a crash, and seems to vanish.

Malice stands with her hands at her sides. She touches her hands to her left arm and the outside of her right thigh and sees the blood on her fingertips. She deduces that the wreckage of the instantly shrunken jet pack must have ricocheted off the force fields.

The Cheshire Cat shouts what looks like "Woo!" but he's on mute.

The Red Queen has stopped running and is staring with her jaw dropped. The surroundings begin to dim and flicker.

The Tinkerer's mouth is hanging open as well. But now she closes it as she meets Malice's eyes. "I say, that was mighty impressive! But how did you know the bouncing jet pack wouldn't injure you…much."

"I didn't, but I was willing to sacrifice myself to commit an act of kindness."

The Red Queen now shakes her head out of her daze and begins running again. The surroundings begin to brighten.

Malice leans her head down and unsquinches her eye to let the monocle plop into her palm. She holds it between her thumb and forefinger as she holds it up. "So, I get to keep this, yeah?"

"What was that?"

"I passed your challenge. I cut the machine free like we agreed in your promise."

The Tinkerer looks surprised for a few moments, but now she grins, says, "Why so you did. You manipulated me masterfully. All due to my Ticktock Heart, I've no doubt. Why, I'm quite proud of myself right now." She appears to be holding herself in a manner that could be described as her hugging herself.

Malice says, "Well I shall be glad to see you really do keep your promises."

"Eh." She flaps her hand dismissively. "Oh, yes, yes, you can keep your trinkets. I shan't take them. As a matter of fact, I'm glad to be rid of that ugly insect. Such a nuisance, he was. But in any case, your turn is over. I shall return shortly. Cheerio."

A press of the button, the square goes blank and black and she vanishes.

Humpty Dumpty

When the Tinkerer returns, she frees the Hatter, who begins to complain so annoyingly that the Tinkerer makes him vanish, "Until he can behave more appropriately."

Alice rolls the dice. And she rolls a ten, does a lot of hopping. She passes start again and lands on the Humpty square.

It begins to fill in with what the Tinkerer refers to as "virtual reality". As she waits, she sets the Vorpal Fist down and picks up the 200 quid she got for passing start.

She sees grass covering the ground and now a hole. It's a grave that looks familiar.

It's Humpty Dumpty's grave!

Alice recalls how she had flung him from a baby chair to be smushed up in the grave. It was an act of kindness to relieve him of his misery. When her heart had turned black she had been proud of killing him. But now she feels conflicted, with her emotions swinging from amused and proud to ashamed and sorry for the poor fellow.

What is wrong with me?

Now she sees something that wasn't there in the original—a podium with a box on top and a button next to the box. On the ground on each side of the podium are two tubes that look like telescopes aimed into the bottom of the grave.

The Tinkerer holds her arms up dramatically. "Behold, what thou hast wrought!"

"Yes, I flung him to his death, but I only did what he asked of me."

"Yes, and then you stole his arms to make wings!"

The Tinkerer nudges with her chin to over Alice's shoulder and with a fright, Alice reaches her hands over her shoulders to see if the arms are still taped there.

I thought I had removed them! Ooh how embarrassing it shall be if they're still there.

But now she sighs in relief as she realizes they aren't there. She says, "Ah, you had me going there."

The Tinkerer giggles. "So I did. You shoulda seen your eyes bug out. I thought they were going to explode." She mimics by bulging her eyes huge and puffing out her cheeks.

"Yes, well I'm glad I got rid of them. It was an awkward phase."

"Yes, and I think you really just forgot about them. So guard cards found them where you'd dropped them. Brought them to me. I put them in with the rest of Humpty's pieces." She makes a crinkled finger gesture at the grave, and Alice, taking the hint, leans over and peers in. And yes, she does see Humpty's arms resting atop the broken shell fragments, and she can also see his legs partially covered by the rubble.

Alice looks down at the eggshells scattered about the bottom of the grave. She feels sorry for him despite how despicable he acted, and she almost wants to cry for him. Indeed, if she would simply allow the tears to well up she could do so easily.

But then she would be making an embarrassing spectacle of herself.

The Hatter is peering down as well while holding his hat on and giggling. "I say, is that Humpty?"

"Yes, I'm afraid so," Alice says.

"What you so afraid of? He looks a bit out of sorts. Did he fall? He always did have a quite unbalanced sort of body. Oblong you see, oblong."

"Unfortunately, I killed him. But I did it to save him from suffering, at least that's what I told myself. And weren't you invisibled?"

The Tinkerer interjects. "Yes, she killed him. But she may be able to remedy that."

The Hatter is still looking down at the shells, with one eye closed, peering. "I say, do you think he might have been the Snark?"

"He doesn't look like a snark," Alice says. To the Tinkerer she says, "How can I fix him? Is that the challenge?"

The Hatter is muttering, "How do you know? Do you know what a snark looks like?"

She shakes her head at him, hoping he'll quiet down.

The Tinkerer says, "Your challenge is merely to make a choice on Humpty's behalf—of heart-havingness versus heart*less*ness."

Meanwhile the Hatter is muttering, "Perhaps *you* are the Snark," referring to Alice.

Alice snaps her head to him to see him pointing at her accusingly—he arches a brow suspiciously.

"What was that?" she snarls.

The Hatter huffs. "I say, it perhaps takes a snark to know what one looks like, don't you think? Therefore, *you* are undeniably the Snark. Case solved. Game over."

"You idiot! How could I be a snark? Do I look like one to you?"

"Since I'm not one, I wouldn't know. Would you?? Hmm??" And here he leans in and peers at her.

She is stricken by the odd out of place notion to kiss him, despite her fury, because she's happy that he's alive enough to even be accusing her. She realizes she's angry at him for not trusting her.

For, I'm not a snark, am I? Perhaps snarks don't realize they're snarks.

She opens her mouth to deny any snarkiness, when the booming sound of the Tinkerer clearing her throat thunders around and indeed, *through* them in the form of tickling vibrations.

"My," says the Hatter, "she must have turned the volume way up on that one, or else the frog in her throat is most exceedingly large."

The Tinkerer points in warning. "Quiet you. You don't want to make me mad, now do you? Do you?!" She glowers at him.

My, what an evil looking child, Alice thinks to herself.

The Hatter swallows hard, shakes his head, and makes a point of (silently) locking with invisible key the point where his two lips meet.

The Tinkerer adds, "I want you to think long and hard before you speak again, as I just might shock you if you prove too intrusive. Understood?"

The Hatter nods.

"Well," Alice says. "That's sorted, then."

The Tinkerer nods. "So, you'll notice the podium and the box. They are part of the challenge. Let's not dilly dally. Open the box or press the button, please. Malice must have her turn as well, you know."

"Yes, I know. So shall I choose which shall be first? Oh, it's like Christmas!"

The Tinkerer rolls her eyes, but giggles despite herself. "Yes, choose."

"I believe I shall go from small to big." And so she opens the small box. Inside, she sees a red cartoonish heart that looks like it was cracked down the middle at some point, but the crack has been sewn together with stitches. "Oh my!" She presses her hand to her mouth in shock.

"I took it from the Queen of Heart's safe, where she had it stored on one of the loooong shelves. She collects hearts, you know, right?"

Alice nods.

"Very good. Now Alice, my dear. I want you to know, that in the grave, those are the actual remains of said Mister Humpty Dumpty, whom you terminated."

Alice bows her head in shame.

"The only part missing is this." She shows Alice a piece of eggshell.

"Eh?"

"But fret not, for with my massive intellect and ingenuity, I have devised a way to reconstruct him, in a manner much more reliable and efficient than using all the King's horses and all the King's men, I might add. However, there is a bit of a catch, a bit of a choice I will present you with. You see, after the Queen of Heart's coup d'etat, I was provided the opportunity to peruse her collection of hearts. And amongst them, I discovered, much to my delight, Humpty Dumpty's original heart." She points at the box with the heart Alice is holding.

Alice gasps. "So does that mean it can be returned to him?" Alice's own heart is racing as she tries to grasp what that might mean.

The Hatter says, "Now if you could only find his brain." He promptly squeals and clamps his hands over his mouth.

The Tinkerer glowers at him, but despite herself, breaks into a chuckle. "Well, okay, that was funny. I'll overlook your occasional remarks, so long as they remain amusing."

Alice, meanwhile, is too lost in thought to be amused.

The Tinkerer considers her. "So about the heart. You have a choice. You might give it to Humpty, you might keep it for yourself…it all remains to be seen."

"Keep it?"

"Yes, perhaps you could use it for your own. It seems quite nice and red, not blackety like your own damaged one. Perhaps you might prefer a transplant. Or you might give it to our Mad Hatter here—he could use one to replace his black one. But you will have the opportunity to speak to Humpty about it yourself."

Alice looks doubtfully at the cluttered mess of shells below. "How—"

"Yes, I know what you're thinking, but I told you about my invention. It is this—a reconstructive algorithm." She points at the tubes aimed at the bottom of the grave.

Alice doesn't know what to say other than "Algorithm?"

The Hatter quips, "Whatever it is, I hope it's got more rhythm than poor dear Alice here—the poor girl can't dance for the life of her."

This elicits a chuckle from the Tinkerer. Alice is rather annoyed.

The Tinkerer explains, "Yes, an algorithm. It's like a computer program, using mathematics and formulas to put all the pieces of the puzzle together in a matter of mere seconds. Because that's what the Humpty fellow is right now, he's like one big jigsaw puzzle, except he's really not even that big. It is simple for the algorithm to figure how to put him together again. I've devised a levitation beam system that will raise all the pieces in the air and assemble them at my command. It's really quite ingenious."

"But what of his heart?"

"Well you may choose to put his heart inside him before he's put together, or leave it out, or choose not to assemble him at all. I shall leave the difficult choice up to you. That is the challenge. But first, I would like you to speak to him, to get his side of things."

The Hatter quips, "His side, I imagine, can only be sunny side *down*, my dear. He's a bit of a grump."

Another chuckle from the Tinkerer, "You're really quite funny."

"Why thank you, milady." He grins charmingly and bows.

"How would I get his side?" Alice asks.

"Quiet simple. Press that button over there. There is a whole history behind Humpty's heart I'm sure you'll find interesting."

Alice eyes the button on top of the podium suspiciously.

The Tinkerer's response: "Go on, then. Have I not played fairly so far?"

Alice realizes that the Tinkerer is in control, and she can actually do anything she wants, even kill anyone at a whim, but so far, she seems intent on playing fairly. So Alice just decides to go ahead and walk over and she reaches out and slaps her palm upon the button. Intense beams of green light shoot out from the lenses of the devices that look like telescopes into the eggshells below.

The devices pivot upward and the eggshell pieces lift as if they're bubbles floating in the air.

Alice hears a humming sound, but she is not sure where it's coming from—from the energy beams or the machines themselves.

Alice gazes, says, "Wow."

"Quiet impressive," the Hatter says, and the Tinkerer shoots him a look to quiet him.

The Tinkerer says, "Now watch as I initiate the algorithm." She presses a button and the pieces of the eggshell cloud begin to twirl and shift in the air. Several seconds pass as the form of Humpty begins to take shape, but the pieces don't fully join together, until now the image of Humpty is presented to them with various cracks and empty spaces where the pieces of him are suspended, but it is as if the pieces of the jigsaw puzzle are held a slight distance away from each other and not fully joined.

"Crikey!" Alice exclaims.

The Hatter claps with a smirk and expression that seems to say, "Look, I'm not speaking." But the Tinkerer does not even glance at him.

The eyes of Humpty slowly open. He looks dazed.

The Tinkerer says, "He exists in a quantum state of in-between, between being fully together and *un*together. In this state he has limited awareness and consciousness —only the purest part of his self will be functioning. Interestingly, that means the part operating higher functioning tasks such as deception will not be functioning. Interestingly, that means he will not lie. You may ask him anything and he will answer truthfully."

The eyes of Humpty open wide in fear and gaze widely around, but he does not even seem to notice Alice and the Hatter standing before him—it is if he is blind. His mouth contorts into an expression of agony, but his arms and legs do not move other than seeming to bob slightly as if they were floating in water.

"Interesting," says the Tinkerer. "In this state of in-between it seems he cannot see. I thought that might be the case."

In a raspy voice that seems wracked with pain and torment, Humpty says, "What…What am I?" He seems not to be speaking to anyone.

Perhaps he is speaking to himself.

"A fat egg," Hatter says, and laughs. "Ow!" he says and twitches. Alice figures the Tinkerer must have shocked him.

The unseeing eyes of Humpty shift toward the Hatter, and now, as if he's a child trying out the speaking of a sound he says, "Oww…owwww."

Alice looks on in concern. "Is he in pain?"

The Hatter waves at the Tinkerer to get her attention and points at himself repeatedly as if to say, "What about me? And *my* pain? I just got shocked!" he pantomimes.

The Tinkerer presses a button and the Hatter disappears. She says, "I'll bring him back later. As for Humpty, I doubt he is aware enough to feel pain in this state of in-between, especially since he doesn't have a heart. He may however, be in discomfort."

Alice pouts a little at that, so the Tinkerer says, "However, we can lessen the time he feels it by moving on to the next part."

Alice arches a brow. "Which is…"

"To help you make your decision, I'd like you to hold his heart inside of him so that you may talk to him that way. You see, there is already an opening—see the missing piece that has been punched out? I've taken to calling it the heart piece."

Humpty moans and his eyes rove about madly, as he says:

I'm Humpty Dumpty, here on my wall!
I'm Humpty Dumpty, and I cannot fall!
…Into love, that is, for it will bring pain,
So I'll just stay heartless and full of disdain.

"Ah," the Tinkerer says, "he's so out of it, he thinks he's still on his wall. How cute. That's the version of the song he would sing to himself when no one was around, I've learned. He doesn't recognize that we're here."

"He doesn't want to fall in love?"

"It seems not. And who would?" She makes a face. "That's how one obtains cooties."

"Well, he doesn't seem to want his heart put in…"

"Yes, isn't that typical of the heartless? But you only need to do it a short while. Come now, be a sport."

"I—I don't know. I have to hold it there?" She feels creeped out by the idea.

"Well, you don't *have* to. But I think it would prove fascinating to speak to a Humpty Dumpty who has a heart, don't you?"

"Heart? No heart!" Humpty shouts.

Alice *does* feel that would be interesting but she gnaws at her lip in worry. "But what if I drop it?"

"Well, then I suppose the decision would be made—Humpty would get his heart back." She flips the piece of eggshell over and over in her hand.

"Okay, what's that then?"

"This is the piece that broke away when the girl punched into his chest and stole his heart."

"Hearts bad!" Humpty says.

Alice gasps. "Why would anyone do that?"

The Tinkerer smirks. "Why, indeed. It's really quite an interesting story. You should ask him about it."

Alice sighs. "Very well then." She approaches the floating, cracked man. The Tinkerer uses her remote to adjust the level of him, so now the hole in his chest is right *there*—she need only hold her arm out straight.

And so Alice takes the heart in her hand and straightens her arm to hold it inside Humpty.

The Tinkerer says, "Alice the stealer of Hearts, feeling any deja vu?"

"Hmm?" Alice says.

The Tinkerer says, "I mean to say, does that position you're in feel familiar?"

Before Alice can respond, her attention is taken away by the feeling of the heart warming up in her hand. She strains her head to peer at it—the inside of Humpty is empty except for her arm and the heart which is now glowing. She feels and sees it shudder, now it begins to beat. She is overcome by wonder.

Holding His Heart in her Hand

Humpty begins to moan as if in pain.

Alice looks at his face—he is frowning. He moans, "Allliiiicceee…" as if the name torments him.

"Yes," she says, "it's me. Can you see me?" She tries to meet his eyes, but his eyes still rove madly about. "Can you hear me?"

He seems to react to that, focusing. "Hear?"

The Tinkerer says, "Perhaps he can recognize how you feel inside him. You've been there before, after all."

This time Alice manages to shoot a quizzical glance at the Tinkerer, who answers it thusly, "I've discovered in my investigations that Humpty has been keeping secrets, secrets about you…"

Alice doesn't know what to make of that. She's distracted by Humpty, who says, "I feel. My heart. Thumping. Pain."

"Oh! Am I holding it too tight?"

"No, other pain. That comes… that comes… from having one… from letting her… you… touch it."

"What do you mean?"

"I can feel you. Inside. I know it's you, Alice, but not you. Like me. I sense…I am…me, but not me."

"Yes." She feels pity well up inside of her. "You are in a state of untogether, in a state of in-between." She doesn't wish to extend his state of wretchedness any longer than necessary. "I want to ask you a question."

"What, you want my heart? Take it. You already stole it, well, you *will* steal it. I'll be killed by her one more time so I must make sure to get it right." Now as if reciting a poem he says, "The times she'll kill me shall be three."

Alice now feels thoroughly confused, "Killed by whom?"

He says, "By you who is not you, the future Alice, but we mustn't tell the before-Alice, must keep it a secret."

Alice looks questioningly at the Tinkerer, who says, "You must understand that he exists now in a state of pure thought—he's untogether, unformed—he may not even perceive himself to even be an entity. He may not even perceive that he and you are two separate people—he may even think that you are just a part of his own mind—like when a person is talking to himself."

"Odd."

"Indeed. Do continue. I know much of it already, but it's delightful to watch how it plays out."

So Alice says to him, "What's the secret?"

"I just told you. You'll kill me three times, according to the prophesy."

"What's the prophesy?"

He says, "It was told to me, thusly:

"The times she'll kill you shall be three,
According to the prophesy.
The third time, by the Vorpal Fist,
To add your heart onto her list."

Alice thinks about it. She realizes she has killed Humpty exactly two times. And with a sickly feeling she gazes at the Vorpal Fist upon the ground. "What happens on the third time?"

"I am saved...or damned. It depends. But don't you know? But no, I can feel." And now he takes a moment, as if trying to sense something. "No, you are the Alice of Before, not the Alice of After, right?"

"Before what?" Alice asks.

The Tinkerer claps and squeals, "Oh, you don't even know! This is delightful!"

He moans, his eyes rove around. "What time is this?"

"The afternoon. Why?"

"Noooo. How old is Alice?"

She is uncertain how to speak to him. He definitely is not experiencing things in a normal fashion. "I... Alice is 13."

"Ah, that is before 18 usually, if time is flowing the normal way. I may be saved."

"What are you talking about?"

"Time...before...future."

Alice sighs. In frustration, she looks to the Tinkerer. "What is he talking about?"

"Time travel. Humpty fell in love with a girl from the future and he traveled back in time because of it."

Humpty moans. "Girl...stealer of hearts."

Alice says, "A girl stole his heart in the future, I mean *will* steal his heart? Oh, it's so confusing. How is that even possible?"

"She showed it to me, before..." Humpty begins to cry...something she'd never seen before, but he'd always been heartless before.

"Oh, dear!" Alice tries to soothe him by stroking his face with her free hand, but he scowls, and shouts, "No! Don't touch me anymore!"

So she stops and looks to the Tinkerer for help.

The Tinkerer says, "The me of the future visited me yesterday. She invented a time travel machine, in the future. She told me what happens in the future to Humpty. A girl stole his heart before he traveled back in time to the present."

"Oh, my! Who would do such a horrible thing."

The Tinkerer smirks. "A girl they will come to call, The girl who will tear your heart out and show it to you before you die."

Humpty reacts to that with a moan. "Aliiiice... noooo..."

She looks at him. "Yes what's wrong?"

"Just take it. End the pain," He says, sounding defeated.

"Take what?"

"My heart. Like before."

A feeling of dread rises inside of Alice. "What are you talking about? I've never..."

Humpty is sobbing and whimpering. "End the pain... the pain."

With a malicious tone in her voice, the Tinkerer says, "That girl in the future who steals all the hearts, who stole *his*, it's you..."

"Me?! How?...Why?!"

Humpty is blubbering to himself, "She took it, but it took away the pain."

The Tinkerer says, "Five years in the future, the 18-year-old version of you allows her heart to grow black. She seduces and breaks the hearts of many in Wonderland. And when she is done toying with them, she pulls their hearts out and shows it to them before they die, using the Vorpal Fist."

"Yes," Humpty whimpers. "Showed it to me. I fell over."

Alice feels ashamed and horrified that she might do such thing in the future, but a part of her doesn't want to believe it and grasps for any holes in the story.

He is sobbing and she suddenly takes pity on him and pulls his heart back out. He immediately stops crying and his face goes blank.

Alice asks the Tinkerer, "But Humpty, how did he get a heart? And a red heart nonetheless? We live in a land of those who are either heartless or blackhearted."

"Yes, we will both be partly to blame. The future-me made a slight miscalculation in my manipulations of time —I caused causation to go slightly backward."

Alice says, "What? What do you mean?"

"*You* caused Wonderland to become blackhearted and heartless, because of what you do in the future."

"Huh? How is that even possible?"

The Tinkerer explains, "Well in my calculations, the future-me mixed up forward and backward at some point. And okay, I'll try to explain it. There are multiple versions of reality, and different versions of you. The future 18-year-old you grew up in a Wonderland where all the creatures had hearts. They were pleasant and kind. But in *that* Wonderland, you let your heart grow black and cruel. You seduced Humpty and others. In *that* Wonderland, Humpty wasn't an egg—he was a boy. But when you stole their hearts, and Humpty used the time machine to travel backward, things got a little wonky. Causation traveled backward and…"

"Wait, what?" Alice says. "You're confusing me."

"Very well. A short lesson. In the normal time stream, there is something called cause and effect. Something causes something else to happen. When time normally moves forward, effects don't happen before their cause, but because of my slight error in the time machine, after you killed Humpty and he used the time machine right after his death, well, causation went *backward* in time. So *your* actions caused all the creatures of Wonderland to become heartless and blackhearted in the past…"

Alice doesn't want to believe it. "That's impossible. Humpty's heart didn't disappear. I have it right here. And I would never…could I?"

"The future 18-year-old you did, and as to how the Queen ended up with his heart in the present, well, it's a bit convoluted and paradoxical, as things tend to be when one alters the timeline."

Alice is shaking her head in a daze. "Me? Seduce? Kill? I would never even, I mean he's an egg!"

"But in the alternate version of Wonderland, he wasn't, but oh, you don't have to believe me. Let's ask him ourselves. In his state of untogether, he won't lie. He doesn't even know what a lie is. Go on, ask him…"

"Humpty?"

"Yes… Whaaat? Aliiice." He seems a lot more grumpy now, but Alice realizes it's because she's taken his heart out.

"Is it true? Did I, will I kill you, in the future?"

He looks around blindly, confused. "Who?"

The Tinkerer suggests, "Use your name, it may help."

So Alice says, "Alice. Will she, did she—ooh, time travel makes it so difficult to say…" She thinks a moment. "18-year-old Alice, did she really pull your heart out?"

He answers, "Yes, broke it, tore it out." And again he repeats that rhyme, "The times she'll kill me shall be three." He doesn't sound sad though—he's stating it matter of fact. But he doesn't have his heart installed, she realizes.

Alice says, "She broke it? Why'd you let her?"

He shrugs. "She was beautiful, on the inside, and I fell in love with her. The only girl I ever let inside. But then she tore out my heart and left me *empty* on the inside. Ah, the irony."

The Tinkerer whispers, "I hate to rush you, but could you move it along? I'll give you a few minutes, then make your choice—assemble him or don't, give him his heart or don't. Thank you."

Alice prods, "You were human once."

"Yes, with a heart, before she stole it, before she killed me a third time."

"But you went back in time, why?"

"To fix things."

"How?"

"It's a secret."

Alice looks to the Tinkerer. "I thought he couldn't lie."

The Tinkerer shrugs. "A secret isn't a lie. I know the secret by the way." She sticks her tongue out at her.

Alice doesn't have time to get mad. She asks him, "What would you fix?"

"A secret," he says.

The Tinkerer giggles and covers her mouth with her hands.

"How did you change to an egg?"

"Alice changed me. 'You're such a pathetic egghead,' she said…when I traveled back in time, an egg is what I became." It was eerie to hear him so calmly say it.

He doesn't seem to feel.

The Tinkerer explains, "When the causation shifted backwards through time, your thoughts rippled through the past. The human Humpty Dumpty was what one would call a nerd. Your cruel last words to him changed things, and when he traveled into the past, an egg-man is what he found he was. After you had killed him."

"Yes, killed me, she did." Again he repeats lines of the poem, "The third time, by the Vorpal Fist."

Alice mutters to herself, "Quoth the raven, nevermore."

The Humpty says mechanically, "Raven was the color of her hair," as Alice says, "He's like the raven in that blasted Edgar Alan Poe poem, always repeating the same thing, but not explaining himself."

"Nevermore shall she hurt me," Humpty says blindly.

Alice huffs. "And he speaks about it all so calmly, like a typical Wonderland heartless jerk. But I've an important decision to make about his livelihood, and I need to hear him speak from the heart." And here, on a whim, she punches her arm out and holds his heart inside him again.

She feels it grow warm and beat as Humpty hisses and his eyes rove madly in pain. "Take it away!" he commands.

"No. Bear with me. I haven't much time. I have an important decision to make. I have the choice of whether to put you together again or not, and if I do, whether to include your heart or not. Do you understand?"

Humpty moans. "Yes, put me together. But leave my heart out. Take it away!"

Alice's brows furrow her forehead. "Why?"

"My heart, it brings me pain. I remember her. I loved her so much, and she broke my heart. I don't want the pain." He begins to cry.

Alice feels such pity for him. "But there were good times, right? You loved her once?"

"Yes, I loved her—there were good times, but then she turned cruel, vicious, betrayal." His voice is filled with misery. He blinks and his eyes focus on her. "I can see. I can see you now."

She smiles at him, but he recoils. He intones,

"She tore out my heart, and then showed it to me.
When I look in your eyes, it is hers that I see.
Assassin of love and the stealer of hearts,
An angel-faced master of boy-breaking arts."

And Alice feels such pity for him, but she can't help but think of the phrase, "it's better to have loved and lost than never to have loved at all." Now she realizes she said that out loud.

Humpty answers, "No, hearts are pain. Take it. Take it far away from me."

But the alternative to a heart, with all the pain it brings, is to be heartless and empty, never to feel, to hurt...or love again, nay, even to remember, deep inside, having ever loved before.

She shakes her head. "I know that may be what you want, but I can't bring myself to do that for you, for without a heart, yes you wouldn't feel the pain, but you wouldn't feel much at all except perhaps anger and hate."

"No, those are my wishes."

"I'm sorry, but I cannot follow them. I only want what's best for you, though you may not understand right now. I will reassemble you—"

He cuts her off. "No! Not with my heart inside!"

Alice feels overwhelming guilt. "I'm so sorry. It's for the best."

"No! Then I choose not to be re-put-together. Let me stay in pieces. Better to be in pieces and dead than to feel that horrible pain of having a heart! It is my wish! *My* life!"

Alice feels tears well up and now she is crying along with Humpty. Perhaps it's best he rest in peace, in pieces, in a pile where he can never be hurt again.

Humpty shouts, "I beg of you!"

And she almost gives in, but now she shakes her head as the warm tears roll and drop. "No," she says, "for despite all the pain a heart brings, it is better to feel something than to not feel at all."

"What are you saying?" Humpty says in a panic. "You're talking nonsense."

Alice looks at the Tinkerer. "I've come to my decision."

"Yes?"

"Put Humpty Dumpty together again, and leave his heart in."

The Tinkerer nods.

Humpty wails, "No! Stop this! It is my wish! Leave me broken!" He awaits her response.

"No," Alice answers, "it's for the best."

And as the Tinkerer fiddles with her remote control, Humpty shouts out, "No! You stupid bitch! Stop this now, or I'll kill you. You hear me?! I'll kill youuuuu!"

With sadness, Alice says, "I hope some day you'll understand. I did this, because I care for you." She looks to the Tinkerer who is watching with questioning eyes, offering Alice the chance to change her mind.

But she nods. The Tinkerer nods back, presses a button. The pieces snap closed as if suddenly pulled back by springs with a whoomp noise. Alice still holds his thumping heart through the hole in his chest where there's the missing piece.

Alice meets his sad eyes, says, "Should I leave the heart in?"

He whispers, "If you do, I will love you…and you will break me…"

Alice can't stand to look in his eyes, she turns her head and lets go of the heart and pulls her arm out.

As Humpty wails, the Tinkerer says, "You pass."

"What?" Alice asks.

"You could have left him dead—he wouldn't have felt anything, or could have left him heartless—still he would have felt nothing. But you chose to revive him with a heart and all the pain it brings, because it is the only way anyone can know love. You did it not out of cruelty, but out of kindness. You pass."

Alice tries to comprehend the words. Wasn't her own heart still partly black? But in any case she feels it grow warm and pleasurable. *Because I committed an act of kindness!* A part of her still hates Humpty but a part still cares about him.

Speaking of Humpty, she now hears his voice, sounding surprised. "Alice? Oh, Alice, it's you! I…care about you!" He sounds surprised.

She spies a glance at him. *He's still an egg, not a man. What does that mean? Will the future still happen?*

The Tinkerer explains, "He has regained full awareness, and now his heart beats within. See it?"

Alice looks into the heart-hole, trying not to meet Humpty's eyes. She sees his heart floating inside, thumping away.

"I shall replace the missing piece soon," the Tinkerer explains.

"I have my heart back?" Humpty asks. "Oh, thank you, whoever did it! I was heartless before."

Alice stares at the ground. "The Tinkerer over there explained to me what I did—the 18-year-old me, in the future. How she broke your heart, and stole it."

He replies, "Yes, 18-year-old you was so beautiful, inside and out. But she let her heart grow black. I tried to save her, but I couldn't. She was the only person I let inside, you know. That's why Malice was inside me—she is like the bad version of you, but she became a part of me because I loved her."

Alice looks at Humpty, puzzled.

He continues. "After 18-year-old you broke my heart, I vowed I would never let myself be hurt by love again. It's *why* I built my wall in the first place—it was symbolic —it was a wall I built to keep people away, and I sat atop it, away from others, while I vowed never to fall... to fall in *love* again."

Alice gasps in shock. "Oh, I'm so sorry 18-year-old me did that to you!"

"Oh, do not apologize my dear. You haven't done those things to me yet."

"And I promise I never shall!"

"You shall kill me three times."

"I shan't!"

"It is prophesied. The number of times is certain, all that can be changed is when."

"Never!"

"I can't change my fate." He laughs sadly. "Oh, my dear, it's the future. Some things can't be changed."

"But some things can! Now that I know these things, I can make sure things don't happen!"

He looks at her affectionately. "But in the future, I loved you. I have those memories. They'll always be a part of me."

Alice nods sadly. "But things will be different. I won't let my heart grow black. I'm already improving. I shan't kill you again, I promise, despite the prophesy. I'll prevent it somehow, I'll get rid of the Vorpal Fist..." Meanwhile Humpty seems to be holding his tongue, fixing her with an expression she can't fathom. Alice's eyes go wide in alarm, as she begins to panic. She looks to the Vorpal Fist—*they said in the future, I killed him with Vorpal Fist—I need to get rid of it.*

She picks the Vorpal Fist up. "Can I return this?" She tries to toss it up over the force field so it will land by the Tinkerer. Except it hits the force field ceiling which flashes green—the fist lands with a clank a short distance away.

As she looks at it, she hears a sinister whisper in her left ear, saying, "Dooo ittt..."

"What?" Alice says.

Humpty and everyone fix her with puzzled looks.

Humpty says, "What?"

The Tinkerer has a strange grin on her face. "You thought that would work?"

Alice suddenly realizes what's going on. She points at the Tinkerer. "Stop it!"

"Hmm?" the Tinkerer says.

"With your virtual reality. Stop the voice in my head."

Again she hears the whisper saying, "He'll hurt you. You must hurt him, and all of them, before they hurt you." She jerks her head. It feels as if it's coming from the glove. *Oh, no.*

She feels a cold sensation in her chest.

"What are you feeling?" Humpty asks, oddly calm, inspecting her.

Alice's mind races frantically, trying to put everything together. "You kept saying—you kept saying, that I would kill you three times."

"Did I?" says Humpty.

Alice gasps as she see the Vorpal Fist move—it rolls over, starts pulling itself by its fingers toward her, whispers, "Hurt him, before he hurts you."

"No!" Alice shouts to Humpty, "I mustn't kill you again! I won't call you an egghead! And I shan't keep that *vile* Vorpal Fist!" She points at it, and it keeps crawling toward her, it whispers, "All's fair in love and warrrrr…"

Humpty is calmly watching the fist crawl.

The Tinkerer says, "Wow, it's like a spider!"

A part of Alice is compelled to run to it, to slip it on, but she knows she must resist that urge. She feels a twitchy feeling in her chest as her heart grows colder. She realizes she must get rid of the Vorpal Fist.

"Humpty, keep that thing away from me. Tinkerer! Please! Take it away!"

The Tinkerer shrugs. "I shan't. Because it must be done.

Alice says, "What are you talking about?!"

Meanwhile Humpty is just watching her calmly. "Why?"

The fist hisses as it crawls closer. "Kill him kill him kill him—tear his heart out!"

Alice is desperate. "Will you remove just the top force field so I can toss it over? Please!"

The Tinkerer nods. "If you wish." She presses a button.

And now Alice knows she must put herself at risk. She must lift up the Vorpal Fist and throw it over the force field—she knows her heart isn't fully black and she might be able to resist the allure of the fist if she's quick about it. She runs toward the fist, lifts it up—as she touches it, the urge to kill surges stronger and the fist hisses, "Tear his heart outttt."—it dazes her for a moment.

She hears Humpty scream in rage to her left and something hits the left side of her face hard. She stumbles into the ground, the Vorpal Fist slides a few feet away.

Humpty is towering over her. "You stupid brat! You wouldn't love me, so I'll force you!"

Alice is horrified. Through her sobs, she can only mutter, "Too young!"

Humpty kicks at her without connecting as she backs away from him on the ground, toward the Vorpal Fist. He follows her with his hand raised to strike again. She rolls over and lunges at the Vorpal Fist—her hand slips into its opening and she feels it latch on like a magnet snapping onto metal. A dark grin stretches her face as she feels her movements become controlled as if by a mind not her own.

She rolls to the side upon the ground—the feeling on her hand within the glove is cold to match her heart. She is out of Humpty's reach now.

He watches her with a stern expression, his stubby hands balled into fists.

Alice, kneeling on the ground, glares at him. She cackles. "Force yourself on me? You pathetic loser. You're not up to the task."

"Sure I am." He raises his fist. He didn't sound convincing. With a war cry, he charges.

Alice stands and runs to meet him, her Vorpal Fist rises up by itself—it effortlessly slips into the hole in Humpty's chest.

They slam into each other. Alice feels the breath knocked out of her, as they bounce off each other. Alice is whirled off her feet. Humpty topples backward off his feet as well.

Alice quickly regains her footing, her movements still don't feel her own—it is as if her heart is guiding them. She sees Humpty lying on his back with cracks and an

Alice-shaped dent in the front. She turns her head and is surprised to see the Vorpal Fist holding a beating heart.

He is weakly trying to stand, looking dazed. Alice grins wickedly as she shows Humpty's heart to him. His eyes are wide with terror as he scooches backward feebly.

Alice says, "Aw, I've left you all empty again." She pouts. Now she shrugs, before tossing the heart away with the flick of her wrist. As Humpty struggles to regain his feet, Alice screams and watches as her arm seems to move on its own, watches as several downward smashes of the Vorpal Fist shatter his face. His arms and legs go limp—his sides and back are still intact but his front has been decimated. She looks over at his hear—it beats three more times and stops.

She stands in stunned silence. She can't bear to look at his body again. She is holding her hands at her sides—the Vorpal Fist slips off and clanks on the ground.

The Tinkerer sniffs. "So you gonna toss that glove over, or what?"

The times she'll kill you shall be three, Alice thinks as she lowers her head in shame.

"I say?!" Tinkerer says.

Alice kneels. With a shout of rage and sorrow, she rises and flings the blood-covered Vorpal Fist up—it sails over the force field wall, landing a short distance from the Tinkerer.

"Alright then," the Tinkerer says, "That's your turn. I shall attend to Malice now."

Alice is enraged. "I just killed him! Don't you care?!"

The Tinkerer arches a brow. "Whom did you kill, hmm?" She nudges her chin at the corpse, but Alice can't bear to look—she never wants to look at him again. The Tinkerer winks, presses a button on the remote and disappears.

Alice shouts, "Damn you! This is not a game!" But it is, and she shall have to wait her turn. She is saddened and angry that she was basically forced to kill Humpty, though a dark part of her is glad that *at least if he's dead, he can't hurt me, can't break my heart.*

She can't bear to look at the corpse, and looks down, but now she sees her arms are covered with dripping bright red blood. *Blood? But there was no blood—he was an empty egg.*

Now out of her peripheral vision she sees there is a lot of bright red...

She turns her head and looks and sees the mangled corpse of a young man, his face is punched in like a caved in mass of mangled meat, a gaping wound is open in his chest.

Alice's mind races as she tries to figure it all out. Somehow the future must have been altered. In the future, he doesn't get turned into an egg. She tries to ponder it more, but it's confusing and makes no sense and will give her a headache if she thinks about it too much.

Maybe in the future, he will never hurt me, and I won't steal his heart.

She picks his heart up. With trembling steps, she approaches the corpse, slips his heart in the hole in his chest. Now she lets the emotion of sorrow flood over her, making sure the tear drops that roll plop onto Humpty Dumpty. Her tears used to have the ability to bring back the dead—she hopes her heart is not too black to mess it up.

After having a good cry, she straightens up on her knees, wipes her tears, and watches expectantly.

It takes a few minutes, but the body starts to glow with a white light. After a few minutes, the flesh begins to shift and heal.

"Curious," Alice mutters as she watches Humpty's healing head. "He's not an egghead!" she exclaims. His head is a regular sort of head on a regular sort of body—the only thing out of place is the hole in his chest through which she can see his heart—and now she sees it begin to thump.

Humpty opens his eyes and fixes her with a handsome grin. "You killed me," he says.

Alice stumbles over her words. "Oh yes, I'm terribly sorry about that. I did revive you."

"Shhh. It's okay, cutie. It's what I wanted. It's why I had to attack you, then force you to react. And for that, *I* am sorry."

She has to look away from his eyes for a moment—they're too intense. "Why?"

"The times she'll kill you shall be three, the third time, by the Vorpal Fist."

"The prophesy?"

"I'm sorry I couldn't tell you. It's why I had to force you to kill me three times, before you turned 18. It's why I had to be so mean to you all these years. And it was why I was so happy the second time you killed me, because I knew I was that much closer to my goal."

"Why? I didn't want to…"

"Don't you see? You were destined to kill me three times, and now that you have, the 18-year-old you doesn't kill me in the future, doesn't call me an egghead. I never became a life-sized egg."

Alice is glad he's not an egg. He's a handsome guy.

He continues, "The 18-year-old you had a fully black heart, so she never gave my heart back, which is why I, and all of Wonderland, became heartless, but the 13-year-old you, you're still sweet and innocent, you *would* give it back, and you did…" He presses his palm over the hole in his chest and grins.

Alice giggles. "You feel it?"

"Oh yes, here…" He reaches and grabs her hand and presses it to his chest.

She can feel it beating, though she avoids actually touching the heart. It feels strange to touch him like this and her hand begins to tremble. Embarrassed, she yanks it away and stares at the ground and says, "So the others in Wonderland. Do they have hearts now too?"

"Of that, I am not certain, but it's possible. Messing about with the timeline can create confusing results."

"I most certainly agree. But I am so glad that you are, a...a result, I mean, I'm glad you're here." On an impulse, she leans in and gives him a peck on the cheek. He looks at her in a way she can't read. "I'm sorry," she says.

"No, it's okay. I—it's just that you're still young. I shouldn't—"

Alice knows that Wonderland characters don't grow older the way she does. "If I were only older..."

"You will be...and I—" He looks away.

"You what?"

"I will come to love you."

"Awww..." Alice feels herself blushing. She feels something like affection for him. Maybe one day she could love him, depending on just how red her heart comes to be.

The Tweedles

Malice gathers up the large ivory six-sided dice and rolls them on the ground.

She shouts, "One and three make four!"

So she hops forward four times on the blank black squares, outlined in glowing green. As she lands on the Tweedles square, the scenery once again expands, she is standing in the dirt beneath the shade of an oak tree, except there is no tree to be seen in the fifteen by fifteen square.

In front of her she sees Tweedledum and Tweedledee combined together as if they're Siamese twins. But the last time she saw them, they were dead—and they were two separate boys.

She arches her brow as she sees.

And they didn't have a deformed third leg in front with one regular leg on the left and another on the right.

She turns her head to the right, where the Tinkerer and other two are watching on.

Malice shouts, "How are they still alive?"

The Tinkerer chuckles. "It's really quite interesting really. Your twin, Alice revived them with her tears. Chose to combine them into a form of Siamese twins, as a means of torturing them, I suppose."

At this prompt, the Red Queen chooses to interject. "Torture? You know what's torture? Running and running and going nowhere. Especially on a treadmill. It's *literally* an exercise in futility. *Literally!*"

Malice says, "Yes, well…" She actually doesn't have anything to say after that—it's simply something one says.

The twins are looking woefully at her. "Can you help us?" says one twin. "Ditto," says the other. "Can you?"

"Help you how?"

"Cut us." "Ditto. Slice."

Malice notices the Cheshire Cat grin even more and bounce around excitedly. She cocks her head from side to side. "You wish to be separated?"

"Yes." The other nods.

The Tinkerer interjects, "Tell her your poem, you dumdums."

They nod, clear their throats, and recite this poem, each taking a turn on a line:

The challenge of this square is this:
To contrive how to cut us in half,
While you leave us both nothing amiss,
And thus give us both reason to laugh,
In the face of death's postponed abyss.

Alice cocks her head. "Why would I be motivated to do such a thing?" She looks at the Tinkerer. "Is there a prize if I succeed?"

"You require a prize? Isn't it good enough to do a good deed?"

Malice considers that. "But what good would that do for me? It doesn't seem logical." But now she is notified that her kindness subroutine has been initiated. *It would be a nice thing to do,* she realizes. *Sometimes one must do nice things even without expecting reward.* Malice cocks her head. After consideration, the kindness subroutine increases the intensity of its activational bias toward altruistic behavior.

Of course, the Tinkerer has heard none of Malice's inner thoughts and continues the conversation. "Very well, how about a prize of…oh! The Vorpal Fist."

Malice says, "Again? It failed to operate for me, previously."

"Yes, but that was when you were heartless. You now have a ticktock heart and I'm curious as to whether it will work now. Tell you what, if you win and it doesn't work, I'll award you 300 quid instead."

It would be logical to commit an act of kindness and also be rewarded for it, on top of that. Malice nods in precise smooth movement. "That would be…agreeable. I accept the challenge."

She peers at the twins and they look back in what Malice construes to be nervousness.

Malice runs her logic algorithms. Within seconds they provide a course of action. She has an x-ray monocle. She must use that to see inside the twins, then use her advanced computational abilities to calculate how to cut them so that exactly 50% goes to each twin while still giving each one his best chance of survival. It will not be a straight cut. That was part of the trick of the riddle, she realizes. A less intelligent being would just cut a straight line down the middle or a diagonal line. But that would most likely prove fatal for one or both twins. So really the best way to cut would be to cut crookedly.

She lifts her x-ray monocle, presses the small button on the top.

And now she can see the insides of the twins, the organs—the expanding and contracting lungs, the swishing blood, the pumping hearts, though she can't tell what color they are—everything looks green. She sees now that all the parts of both twins are there, smushed and tangled together but if the cuts are precise they can be cut free.

And she is nothing if not precise.

"Stay still," she says to the twins.

They nod, then take in a breath and hold it.

Malice uses her calculations to guide her. Her hands glide like a machine, quickly cutting and tugging at flesh to reach deeper regions as the crackle sound and smell of burned flesh rises in the air.

The twins whimper but manage to remain still.

As Malice cuts down their torso region she says, "Curious that the laser seals off nerves as it cuts. You won't even feel what you refer to as pain. And there will be no bleeding as well."

She doesn't expect them to respond. As she cuts along their backs, she says, "Shh. It shall be over soon." Her comforting behavior database informs her that saying shhh...can prove soothing to humanoid beings and many mammals.

Finally the twins fully separate.

"There, it is done," she says. Humans tend to appreciate and expect such announcements, according to her database. "You shall have to get new outfits, but that shouldn't be hard."

She is standing behind them. Smoke is still rising from their bodies. She watches as they look down at themselves then at each other and grin and laugh and hug while awkwardly holding their tattered clothes in place. "We are free!" says one. "Ditto! Completely ditto!"

They are patting each other on the backs as they hug.

Malice's kindness subroutine gives her a notification that it is a heartwarming moment, so she sighs and makes the movement to wipe a tear from her eye. She says, "Awah!" Of course, there is no tear, but at least she made the effort, which her database informs her, is often most important to biological humans.

"So how it feel to do good deed?" Tinkerer asks.

"Heartwarming," Malice says. "Awah!"

"Is it?"

"It's just a figure of speech."

The twins are sobbing now, hugging. One says, "I shall never strike you again!" "Ditto, unless you strike me first." "Which I shan't." "And I shan't neither." "And I more likely, shan't." "Eh? I *most definitely* shan't. More than you." He glares playfully at his brother, then smiles.

But on to other things. Malice looks at the Tinkerer. "My prize?"

"Oh, yes, quite." A pedestal rises from the ground with the Vorpal Fist atop it.

As Malice picks it up, the Tinkerer proclaims "Behold, the Vorpal Fist!"

Malice notes that the fist is covered in fresh, bright red blood. *Perhaps this is a most desirable weapon,* she thinks as she slips it on.

But it is overly slippery, and much too big for her hand, and slips off again. She peers at the Tinkerer, says, "Explain."

"Well, it seems it won't work for you, though I thought there was a chance it might. It seems to only work for those whose hearts are at least a little black, and you have a ticktock heart, and the fist only tears out the hearts of others who feel love for the wearer, and no one loves you."

Malice's programs notify her that being unloved should make her sad. "That is a saddening thing," she says.

The Tinkerer peers at her curiously. "Indeed. Perhaps it's best that the fist be hidden away. Do you agree?"

"Yes," Malice says. "It is an unkind weapon. It is best for it to be hidden or even destroyed."

The Tinkerer grins. "Excellent! That is a most benevolent decision. You pass."

Malice doesn't respond.

"Of course, your social skill programming could use some improvement. Hmm. In any case, won't you give the fist to the twins? They'll carry it away."

"Very well," Malice says and hands it to the twins.

"Thank you." "Likewise." They grin and look like sweet boys.

Malice practices her smile on them. They give her a curious look.

They disappear and the square turns plain and black.

The Tinkerer says, "So you just committed two, count them, *two* good deeds! How do you feel about that?"

"They both fell satisfactorily inside the desired kindness parameters."

"How does your heart feel? Warm at all, tingly, twitchy?"

"Why? Is it malfunctioning?"

"Never mind. That's your turn," says the Tinkerer, now she disappears as well, leaving 300 quid on the ground.

BaCK to StarT

Alice giggles at what Humpty just said.

On her right, Alice sees the Tinkerer pop back into view and say, "I'm back! It's your turn again!"

Alice and Humpty chuckle awkwardly.

"Oh," the Tinkerer says, "did I interrupt a moment?" She shrugs.

The Cat makes smoochy kissy faces in his containment field.

Alice explains, "I brought him back to life and—"

The Tinkerer waves her hand. "Yes, yes, my theory proved to be correct. I fixed Wonderland. You're welcome. But time's a-wastin'. Say your goodbyes."

Alice frowns. "Goodbyes?" She sees Humpty begin to smile, but then he disappears.

"Roll the dice please," the Tinkerer says.

Alice rolls them. 11. She hops.

As she lands on the square, she sees she's back at the start square. It expands into a plain square with "Start" on the ground.

"Well," Alice says, "I've ended up back at the start. Rather boring."

"Now you know how I feel," remarks the Red Queen.

Alice tries not to scowl at her in irritation. Instead she says, "Yes, this is the start square, so there is no challenge."

"Nor is there a snark," the Hatter says, "or is there?"

Apparently, the Hatter has been turned back on again. "What does *that* mean?" Alice asks.

The Hatter shrugs.

The Tinkerer says, "The good news is that when you land on, or pass the start square, you are rewarded with 200 quid." She presses a button, and coins appear on the floor.

Alice notices the Cat blowing a silent raspberry at her.

Alice looks down. "Your game is most confusing, what am I to buy with these quids?"

"Perhaps you could buy a clue," the Hatter quips.

"Hush, you," says Alice.

"There are certain squares," says the Tinkerer, "where you may buy objects. So save your quid."

"She can't even save her breath, though I wish she would," says the Hatter.

Alice glares at him. She shoots another glare at the Cheshire Cat, who is silently laughing in his containment field.

The Tinkerer says, "In any case, that's your turn." And she and the other two disappear.

Shadow

Malice rolls the dice. She rolls a 7, and while multiple cartwheeling precisely, passes start again for another 200 quid and ends up on the square labeled, Shadow.

She picks up the quid and the square expands and begins to fill in. She sees two girls bent over, held in some sort of guillotine with gravelly ground beneath. When it fills in more, she can see all things clearly now.

On the left, she sees her shadow projected onto a white screen. Her shadow is bent over in a guillotine that is entirely made of shadows, all except for the multicolored blade which is suspended above—upon closer inspection, she sees that the blade is actually a small rainbow. To the right of her shadow is a paper cut-out doll of Malice/Alice bent over in a paper guillotine. The paper doll is smaller than life size, but because of the angles and distance, the projected shadows are life-sized. A mechanical lamp is on the right of the dolls, providing light. The rainbow blade seems to be coming from a block of glass or crystal that's suspended above the paper doll, as if levitated.

Malice arches a brow. "Curious."

Her shadow says, "Hello Malice."

Malice arches her other brow. "So you're speaking to me again?" Her shadow had recently decided she no longer wanted to be the shadow of either Alice or Malice.

The Tinkerer interrupts, as she has a tendency to do. "I've apprised her of your situation. She knows you now have a heart. She has volunteered to be guillotined if you decide so."

Malice says, "Volunteered?"

"Yes, I convinced her to give you two another chance. Because Alice's heart is no longer fully black and she is on the path to potential recovery and you have a kindness-equipped heart. So I approached your shadow with my idea, and she agreed. But the choice is up to you. That's what this square is about."

The shadow says, "That's right. Let's see how your Ticktock Heart guides."

Malice says, "So I surmise you're not a prisoner?"

"You surmise correctly. I'm holding my head here of my own free will, because—well, I shall allow the Tinkerer to explain."

Malice turns to the Tinkerer, who says, "Very well. It all started when I began to ponder your and Alice's condition. Your shadow had abandoned you both. She was quite upset with you."

"Quite!" the shadow chimes.

The Tinkerer continues, "Even if she wasn't, there was the problem that there was only one of her between the two of you. Would she choose to be the shadow of one of you? Would she switch back and forth between you two? It was a conundrum that I found intriguing. But after a bit of thought and research, I came up with a solution, due to my massive intellect and ingenious inventiveness." She takes a moment to pause and grin in her self-satisfaction.

"Hey! I helped!" the shadow shouts.

"Ah, of course. I called your shadow forth using the paper cutout and she informed me about the various aspects of shadows."

The shadow says, "I only helped because she said she'd be able to make you two be respectable and pleasant again. Girls I could be *proud* to be the shadow of again."

The Tinkerer says, "And I have done so. In any case, I figured out the solution—a rainbow blade to slice your shadow into two parts. Each of you would get a part. She informed me that, over time, the two parts of her would regenerate."

"My, how curious." Malice's kindness subroutine instructs her to be sensitive to her shadow's feelings, so she says to her, "But won't being beheaded be unpleasant?"

"A little bit, probably. I'm not looking forward to it. But it won't be that bad. Like ripping off a bandage, I expect. But I'll do it for you two."

"That would be most kind of you." Malice bows. "But why a beheading?"

"Well, it's not the most desirable," says her shadow. "She can explain better."

The Tinkerer says, "It takes a great deal of effort to create the proper prism for a rainbow blade powerful enough to cut your shadow. Since you're Malice and Alice, your shadow is very strong and has special abilities beyond those of an ordinary shadow. Why, it would even be able to disrupt the Red Queen's laser down there." She points at the red light projecting from the bottom of the treadmill. "It's a good thing you're on the other side of that force field. But never mind that. Only a very special kind of rainbow can cut your shadow apart. I was only able to create a rather small one, and once the rainbow blade is used, it disappears and the prism becomes useless. But the blade is a sufficient width to cut a narrow body part—such as the neck. It's the obvious choice. Your shadow assures me that beheading is not fatal for the Flat Ones and everything will eventually grow back."

Malice says, "I see. And I would decide who would get which part?"

"Yes, you would choose heads or tails, as it were. Or you may choose neither, in which case, I'll happily destroy the prism and send the shadow on her way to wherever it is shadows go when you cannot see them."

"And I shan't have the shadow all to myself?"

"That is not an option, no."

"What if—"

"Before you try to bribe me or threaten me or plead, I assure you, nothing will sway me. It is *not* one of the choices."

Malice closes her mouth and nods. "Very well. Let us consider our choices then. Am I so petty that I would choose for *neither* of us to have a shadow rather than have to share? Perhaps that is the choice the heartless version of me would have made. She had little use for shadows anyway. But I've had a change of heart." She chuckles. "I made a joke there."

"I noticed," says the Tinkerer. "You needn't remark on every joke. It can diminish them."

"Point noted. In any case, my kindness subroutine has notified me that 'caring is sharing', therefore I wish to share with my twin."

"Right on ya!" says the shadow.

"So," Malice continues, "that leaves the matter of who shall get what portion. Am I correct in thinking that the head will be able to speak, but the body will not?"

"That is correct," says the shadow. "That is, until the body grows a new head."

Malice nods. "So which is the better part? Or can such a notion not be quantified? Perhaps, each part has its benefits. For example, with the arms part of the shadow,

I would be able to form shadow puppets to amuse myself, correct?"

"Yes," says the shadow.

"Very well," Malice says. "Making shadow puppets is something I should like to do soon. I would like to make bunnies. So I choose the non-head body part. I shall have to wait for the head to grow."

"Ah!" says the Tinkerer. "So that's your decision."

"Yes, definitely."

The Tinkerer nods.

The shadow says, "It's been a pleasure speaking with a kinder you. I look forward to being your shadow again."

"Thank you."

"Okay," says the Tinkerer, "here we go."

"Let's do this," says the shadow, trying to sound brave. "Do it right quick. Less pain. Take it right off."

"Off with her head!" the Tinkerer shouts. She presses a button, and the prism and the rainbow guillotine blade descend. The shadow of her head falls and rolls upon the ground. The muted Cheshire Cat is bouncing excitedly, and the Red Queen just keeps running, seemingly unaffected.

Malice looks to the paper Alice cutout to see that her head has been shorn off as well.

How curious.

And now the shadow head begins to roll. The headless shadow body rises to stand upon its feet. The shadow head rolls past the green line, rises up to face the

Cheshire Cat for a few moments and disappears. The Cat looks momentarily creeped out.

The headless shadow stands behind Malice and elongates itself at an angle, looking like a right and proper shadow should look (at least from the neck down).

Now Malice quickly jumps into action, setting her plan into motion. Her algorithms are able to calculate the precise angles, according to the light source, to attain the exact positioning for her shadow. She runs to the lamp, grabs it. The lamp isn't hot at all—perhaps because it's a virtual lamp. She turns it to direct the light toward the Red Queen, slightly to the right of her. The Red Queen looks puzzled, but keeps running.

Malice hopes she can move fast enough to maintain the element of surprise. The second part of her plan is this: she runs to stand in front of the lamp, the light on her body forms an elongated headless shadow on the ground that extends past the boundaries of the square. She's already calculated the exact position to stand. Her long drawn out headless shadow stands beside the laser beam. She presses her arms together so they form what look like large shadow-scissors being held open. She moves the scissors over the laser beam…and closes them, causing that part of the laser beam to be shrouded in shadow.

She holds her hands still, not sure if it will work. But the surroundings around her begin to flicker. Now they fade. Now the virtual reality square disappears entirely, and Malice finds herself in a room that seems eerily familiar. Some people are standing next to her. She sees a looking glass in front of her, but of course she doesn't have a reflection. She sees the Mad Hatter's reflection next to her though, and the Red Queen's and the Cat's reflections who for some reason appear to be behind her.

GaMe OVeR

Malice now realizes she's in the Looking Glass Room. She turns around to see the Tinkerer, Cat and Red Queen. The Cat no longer appears to be surrounded by his containment field.

The Red Queen laughs insanely and launches herself off her treadmill and runs out of the room.

It just gets curiouser and curiouser, Malice thinks to herself.

Alice and the Mad Hatter are looking about as if confused.

Meanwhile, the Tinkerer meets Malice's eyes, and says, "Very good. You pass."

Malice says, "You set me up again?"

And Alice is saying, "What's going on?"

The Cheshire Cat, realizing he is no longer contained, says, "I'm out of here!" And floats out of the room.

The Hatter says, "This place could use a dusting."

"Ladies and gentleman," says the Tinkerer, "we are coming to the end of our journey. My apologies Malice, if you feel I manipulated you. I was honestly curious as to whether you would figure it out."

"Curious," Malice snides back.

"But you performed splendidly. You figured out the puzzle I set up for you. Granted, you shall never be as intelligent as me, but I'm proud, nonetheless."

The Hatter is rubbing his chin while peering at Alice.

Alice is indignant, says, "I said, I'm not the Snark! Now quit looking at me! Can't you see our surroundings have changed? There's more pressing matters!"

"Yes," interjects the Tinkerer, "you are now inside the Looking Glass House. Well, technically, you were here all along, but the virtual reality disguised it. Once the laser was interrupted, the prism no longer shined its light into the mirror."

Alice says, "Lasers are those light thingies right?"

The Hatter turns to face Malice. "Aha! Finally you show up. How convenient. It will surely turn out that it is *you* who are the Snark after all!" And he glares at her with an accusing finger pointed at her.

As he turned, Malice's precise eyes and calculating mind picked up on an anomaly in the movement of the hat atop the Hatter's head, as if something *beneath* the hat shifted weight ever-so-slightly. A typical person would never have noticed, but Malice has the eyes of a computer-aided genius of physics. She stares at his hand and says,

**"Be careful what you hunt for,
You mightn't like what you will find,
When you point one finger forward,
Three fingers point behind."**

"What's that?" the Hatter says, glancing at his hand and now lowering it defensively, even trying to hide it behind his back.

Malice's eyes crinkle. "Mister Mad Hatter. Fancy meeting you here. But 'tis a pleasure." She curtsies, hoping she can get him to tip his hat, or if he doesn't, that would prove quite suspicious wouldn't it?

He sneers—does not bow or tip his hat. "If this is your pleasure, I should like to see your pain."

Malice tries her smile again. "Oh come now. I'm sorry for killing you. But it's all sorted now. I've got a kindness-equipped heart now, and wish to express my condolences."

He folds his arms. "You did a poor job of killing me. You did not, even, for here I stand."

Malice attempts to be charming. "Oh, come now. I'm sorry. We can begin anew. I'll try to make it up to you. Won't you at least tip your hat to me, at least as a beginning?"

Alice looking on says, "What are you two going on about?"

Malice curtsies. "A tip of the hat?"

The Hatter crosses his arms tighter and looks away. "I shan't tip my hat to a snark with such an unfortunate appearance. Talk about *Wonder*land. I *wonder* how you *landed* on your face so hard. Hrmph!"

Alice asks, "Are you two having a tiff or something?"

Meanwhile, Malice thinks, *Enough of this silliness.* Without a word, she lifts the x-ray monocle to her eye and peers at the hat.

And she sees, underneath the hat, a tentacled squid-like creature. The creature is upside down, with its mouth attached to the top of the Hatter's head. The creature has squished its body inside the hat—it would be a wonder if it is actually comfortable.

Malice arches a brow. "How curious."

"What is?" says Alice.

The Hatter says, "Curiousity killed the cat. Eight times. Why not ask the idiot. And that monocle does not agree with your face, but then your face has arguments with everything."

Malice ignores his diversion. She lowers the monocle and points at the Hatter's hat. "There is a strange sort of creature residing beneath his hat, locked onto his head, like a leach. I suspect it is a parasite, or may even be in control of the Hatter's body."

"Ha!" The Hatter laughs. "That's what I'd expect a snark to do. Accuse someone else to take attention away from herself!"

"Then why not lift your hat and prove me wrong?"

"I have hat head. You shan't see. Would be much too embarrassing!"

"Is it true?" Alice says.

Malice says, "So, perhaps I am the snark, yes, but why don't you simply remove your hat?"

"Ha! I don't take orders from you. Why, you couldn't even order a fist sandwich because it would be too afraid to touch your ugly face."

And Alice is watching on with her head pressed to her mouth saying, "Is it true, Hatter?"

Meanwhile, the Tinkerer watches on calmly.

Malice stamps her foot. "Enough of this. There is obviously a creature under your hat. It can't be denied any longer. So show yourself, creature!"

"Oh, you!" the Hatter shouts. He carefully pulls his hat from off his head. With a suction sound, a moist squidlike creature slides from the hat and remains clinging to the top of the Hatter's head. The tentacles on top fan out and sway. Glassy black eyes peer out near the top of the Hatters head, where the mouth of the creature is latched on. The Hatter's mouth speaks, saying, "Happy now? Yes, I am the Snark, and the Hatter is my host. I was doing what a snark does, drawing attention away from myself by attacking and insulting others. But you ruined it!"

Malice's empathy subroutine kicks in. "Forgive me. I must try to see it from your perspective," she says.

Alice shouts, "Let go of him!"

The Hatter's face looks at Alice and holds his hand up. "Ah, ah, let me say my piece. This is the important moment I've been leading everything up to, and I know it's hard for you, but if you can manage to keep your mouth shut for just a moment, you just might learn something. Now, *listen:*

**"I'll tell you the true danger,
And I mean this symbolically,
The Snark is not a stranger.
The Snark is you and me."**

The Hatter's body steeples its hands, with the wriggling creature writhing atop his head. He meets the eyes of everyone in the room and gives it a moment for his words to sink in. Finally, he says, "Now what do I mean by that? Hmm? And now we come the lesson I've been *trying* to teach you all along. It is this…we are *all* snarks, on the inside, no matter how much we try to hide it, or fight it. Yes, I am obviously the Snark, but…so are you." He points at the Tinkerer. "I've heard some of your snide comments." The Tinkerer looks down. "And you're the Snark." He points at Malice, who arches a brow. He points at Alice. "And yes, even you are the Snark, Alice."

Alice moves quick. Shrieking, she runs and punches the Snark with a sick squishy sound. The Snark and Hatter's head lurch to the side.

The Snark screeches and flails in anger. The Hatter's mouth yells, "You gormless nitwit!"

Alice punches the Snark again with a squishy sound, and shouts, "I know you are!"

Malice is wondering if she should feel sorry for the Snark. She is accessing her database.

The Snark wriggles and the Hatter's head begins to cry and says, "Quit being mean! I'm just doing what a good parasite does, and I've done good for my host. I fixed him up, repaired his neck, made him good as new!"

"Well, go parasite somewhere else!" Alice shouts. She shakes her fist threateningly. "Let him rest in peace!"

The Hatter's face says, "Oh, very well! *This* parasite shall not miss the pair-of-sights of you two'ses ugly face. I bid you good day!" And with a piercing screech, it launches from atop the Hatter's head, landing on the ceiling, where it clings like a spider. The Hatter's body crumples to the floor. The Snark, meanwhile, skitters across the ceiling, breaks a window and scurries away.

FINALE

Alice scowls at the Tinkerer. "You knew!"

The Tinkerer says, "Of course I knew. I tried to fix him and his broken neck, but it was beyond my abilities. The Snark was able to repair him."

The Hatter sits up and says, "Repair who? Or is it whom?"

Malice says, "Whom."

Alice shouts, "You're alive!"

The Hatter's eyelids flutter. "Why so I am. Ah! Don't kill me!"

Alice soothes, "Don't worry. I shan't. My heart is much redder now." She looks down at the top of the Hatter's head. It's a bit messy, gory even, so she says, "Why don't you put your hat back on?"

Vacantly he nods, looks at Malice. "How about you? Gonna kill me?"

"No, I have a mechanical heart now, that makes me be kind." As he puts on his hat, she walks over to him, she pats him on the shoulder and says, "There there."

He looks up at her, "Eh? I say, where am I? How did I get here?"

The Tinkerer explains, "In order to use the Hatter as a host, the Snark had to repair the damage done to him. See? It all worked out. Because of me, the Hatter is fixed."

Alice meanwhile is pondering the Hatter as Malice takes his hand and helps lift him up to stand.

Alice says, "So what about you, Hatter? Have you got a heart?"

The Hatter greets her with a puzzled frown. "Why, whatever do you mean? Of course I do, don't I?" He presses his hand to his chest. "Why yes, there it is!"

Alice says, "What color?

The Hatter says, "Well, I can't see it. But red, I assume."

Alice grins big.

Malice arches a brow.

The Tinkerer says, "My, what a happy ending this is turning out to be, but perhaps *this* ending is all a dream from which you will awaken only to find yourself back in the horrible version of Wonderland."

They all look at her in worry, except for Malice, who finds the notion intriguing.

"Just joshing ya," the Tinkerer says.

Malice says, "So I found the Snark. What's my prize?"

Meanwhile, Alice kisses Hatter on the cheek, says, "I'm glad you're alive."

The Hatter says, "Thank you," and begins to blush.

"Aw, how sweet," says the Tinkerer. She looks at Malice. "Your prize is, you get to choose."

"Choose what?"

The Tinkerer sweeps her arm to the mirror. "Ladies and gentleman, I present to you, the portal from Wonderland into the outside world. It is the same one you have been working hard to travel through, but I have made some alterations. You see, before, in order for you to travel through it, you needed a reflection. It is why I created a clone of Malice to see if she could use the clone as a reflection substitute, but things have changed. I've coated the Looking Glass with my special one-way mirror treatment so that now, only those *without* a reflection can travel through."

Alice gasps. "Oh my!"

Malice arches a brow, says, "Intriguing."

Hatter says, "Like a vampire!"

And the Tinkerer continues, "So, since only one of you, either Malice or Alice, can go through the mirror, a choice must be made as to who will accompany me."

Malice arches a brow. "The choice is simple. The outside world is not my world. I belong here. Alice should go." She looks at Alice. "Is that okay?" She smiles.

Alice presses her hand to her chest and feels her heartbeat quicken. "Oh my! It's everything I've wanted, my dream come true! Oh, thank you thank you!" The tears come now. She and the Hatter hug. He's crying too.

Now Malice and Alice hug.

Malice says to the Tinkerer, "I'm curious. How is it that you will be able to go through the mirror?"

"Oh me? I am actually the reflection of my other self. She is back in the outside world, doing whatever she's doing. But we shall join up soon. And I shall leave you in charge." She hands the remote control to Malice. "Malice, with this remote will come great power. With the Queen of Hearts in the dungeon, I am certain you will be a just and kind ruler, because of your mechanical heart and kindness subroutine."

Malice bows. "As long as they function properly, I'm sure I will be the nicest of rulers."

The Tinkerer waves her hand. "Eh? Well of course they'll function properly. I designed them." She hugs Malice's legs. "Now that I've fixed Wonderland, I'm so looking forward to getting back to the outside world, and playing with you, Alice." She walks over to her and hugs the lower part of her poofy dress.

Alice pats the top of her head. "Hmm? What do you mean play with me?"

"You know, games. The typical things."

"Hmm? Are we to be together? Will we even live in the same area? What of your family?"

"Oh yes, Mum and Dad will be so glad to see you!"

"What do you mean? Are you to adopt me?"

"Oh!" The Tinkerer giggles. "Don't you know? I thought I had mentioned it. Alice! I'm your sister."

Alice laughs. "Oh, you scamp! Why didn't you say so?"

"I thought I did! Or perhaps it slipped my mind. In any case, yes, I came over to find you and bring you back so I could have my big sister to play with."

Alice kisses the top of her head.

And so the end of Alice's long stay in Wonderland approaches.

O frabjous day! Callooh! Callay!

The Cheshire Cat reappears and Alice gives him a goodbye rub beneath his floating chin as he purrs.

Tears flow freely as she hugs the Hatter and Malice, waves and takes her little sister's hand, and now, hand in hand, she and her little sister walk through the Looking Glass into the world beyond.

51284729R00146

Made in the USA
Middletown, DE
10 November 2017